T

Se

of

Father Brown

G.K. Chesterton

Written by G. K. Chesterton
1874 – 1936

First published in 1927
By Cassell & Co, London

This edition published 2022
By Affordable Classics

To Father John O'Connor, of St. Cuthbert's Bradford,
Whose truth is stranger than fiction,
With gratitude greater than the world.

I: THE SECRET OF FATHER BROWN

FLAMBEAU, once the most famous criminal in France and later a very private detective in England, had long retired from both professions. Some say a career of crime had left him with too many scruples for a career of detection. Anyhow, after a life of romantic escapes and tricks of evasion, he had ended at what some might consider an appropriate address: in a castle in Spain. The castle, however, was solid though relatively small; and the black vineyard and green stripes of kitchen garden covered a respectable square on the brown hillside. For Flambeau, after all his violent adventures, still possessed what is possessed by so many Latins, what is absent (for instance) in so many Americans, the energy to retire. It can be seen in many a large hotel-proprietor whose one ambition is to be a small peasant. It can be seen in many a French provincial shopkeeper, who pauses at the moment when he might develop into a detestable millionaire and buy a street of shops, to fall back quietly and comfortably on domesticity and dominoes. Flambeau had casually and almost abruptly fallen in love with a Spanish Lady, married and brought up a large family on a Spanish estate, without displaying any apparent desire to stray again beyond its borders. But on one particular morning he was observed by his family to be unusually restless and excited; and he outran the little boys and descended the greater part of the long mountain slope to meet the visitor who was coming across the valley; even when the visitor was still a black dot in the distance.

The black dot gradually increased in size without very much altering in the shape; for it continued, roughly speaking, to be both round and black. The black clothes of clerics were not unknown upon those hills; but these clothes, however clerical, had about them something at once commonplace and yet almost jaunty in comparison with the cassock or soutane, and marked the wearer as a man from the northwestern islands, as clearly as if he had been labelled Clapham Junction. He carried a short thick umbrella with a knob like a club, at the sight of which his Latin friend almost shed tears of sentiment; for it had figured in many adventures that they shared long ago. For this was the Frenchman's English friend. Father Brown, paying a long-desired but long-delayed visit. They had corresponded constantly, but they had not met for years.

Father Brown was soon established in the family circle, which was quite large enough to give the general sense of company or a community. He was introduced to the big wooden images of the Three Kings, of painted and gilded wood, who bring the gifts to the children at Christmas; for Spain is a country where the affairs of the children bulk large in the life of the home. He was introduced to the dog and the cat and the live-stock on the farm. But he was also, as it happened, introduced to one neighbour who, like himself, had brought into that valley the garb and manners of distant lands.

It was on the third night of the priest's stay at the little chateau that he beheld a stately stranger who paid his respects to the Spanish household with bows that no Spanish grandee could emulate. He was a tall, thin grey-haired and very handsome gentleman, and his hands, cuffs and cuff-links had something overpowering in their polish. But his long face had nothing of that languor which is associated with long cuffs and manicuring in the caricatures of our own country. It was rather arrestingly alert and keen; and the eyes had an innocent intensity of inquiry that does not go often with grey hairs. That alone might have marked the man's nationality, as well the nasal note in his refined voice and his rather too ready assumption of the vast antiquity of all the European things around him. This was, indeed, no less a person than Mr. Grandison Chace, of Boston, an American traveller who had halted for a time in his American travels by taking a lease of the adjoining estate; a somewhat similar castle on a somewhat similar hill. He delighted in his old castle, and he regarded his friendly neighbour as a local antiquity of the same type. For Flambeau managed, as we have said, really to look retired in the sense of rooted. He might have grown there with his own vine and fig-tree for ages. He had resumed his real family name of Duroc; for the other title of "The Torch" had only been a title de guerre, like that under which such a man will often wage war on society. He was fond of his wife and family; he never went farther afield than was needed for a little shooting; and he seemed, to the American globe-trotter, the embodiment of that cult of a sunny respectability and a temperate luxury, which the American was wise enough to see and admire in the Mediterranean peoples. The rolling stone from the West was glad to rest for a moment on this rock in the South that had gathered so very much moss. But Mr. Chace had heard of Father

Brown, and his tone faintly changed, as towards a celebrity. The interviewing instinct awoke, tactful but tense. If he did try to draw Father Brown, as if he were a tooth, it was done with the most dexterous and painless American dentistry.

They were sitting in a sort of partly unroofed outer court of the house, such as often forms the entrance to Spanish houses. It was dusk turning to dark; and as all that mountain air sharpens suddenly after sunset, a small stove stood on the flagstones, glowing with red eyes like a goblin, and painting a red pattern on the pavement; but scarcely a ray of it reached the lower bricks of the great bare, brown brick wall that went soaring up above them into the deep blue night. Flambeau's big broad-shouldered figure and great moustaches, like sabres, could be traced dimly in the twilight, as he moved about, drawing dark wine from a great cask and handing it round. In his shadow, the priest looked very shrunken and small, as if huddled over the stove; but the American visitor leaned forward elegantly with his elbow on his knee and his fine pointed features in the full light; his eyes shone with inquisitive intelligence.

"I can assure you, sir," he was saying, "we consider your achievement in the matter of the Moonshine Murder the most remarkable triumph in the history of detective science."

Father Brown murmured something; some might have imagined that the murmur was a little like a moan.

"We are well acquainted," went on the stranger firmly, "with the alleged achievements of Dupin and others; and with those of Lecocq, Sherlock Holmes, Nicholas Carter, and other imaginative incarnations of the craft. But we observe there is in many ways, a marked difference between your own method, of approach and that of these other thinkers, whether fictitious or actual. Some have spec'lated, sir, as to whether the difference of method may perhaps involve rather the absence of method."

Father Brown was silent; then he started a little, almost as if he had been nodding over the stove, and said: "I beg your pardon. Yes. . ... Absence of method. . . . Absence of mind, too, I'm afraid."

"I should say of strictly tabulated scientific method," went on the inquirer. "Edgar Poe throws off several little essays in a conversational form, explaining Dupin's method, with its fine links of logic. Dr. Watson had to listen to some pretty exact expositions of Holmes's method with its observation of material details. But nobody seems to have got on to any full account of your method. Father Brown, and I was informed you declined the offer to give a series of lectures in the States on the matter."

"Yes," said the priest, frowning at the stove; "I declined."

"Your refusal gave rise to a remarkable lot of interesting talk," remarked Chace. "I may say that some of our people are saying your science can't be expounded, because it's something more than just natural science. They say your secret's not to be divulged, as being occult in its character."

"Being what?" asked Father Brown, rather sharply.

"Why, kind of esoteric," replied the other. "I can tell you, people got considerably worked up about Gallup's murder, and Stein's murder, and then old man Merton's murder, and now Judge Gwynne's murder, and a double murder by Dalmon, who was well known in the States. And there were you, on the spot every time, slap in the middle of it; telling everybody how it was done and never telling anybody how you knew. So some people got to think you knew without looking, so to speak. And Carlotta Brownson gave a lecture on Thought-Forms with illustrations from these cases of yours. The Second Sight Sisterhood of Indianapolis — — "

Father Brown, was still staring at the stove; then he said quite loud yet as if hardly aware that anyone heard him: "Oh, I say. This will never do."

"I don't exactly know how it's to be helped," said Mr. Chace humorously. "The Second Sight Sisterhood want a lot of holding down. The only way I can think of stopping it is for you to tell us the secret after all."

Father Brown groaned. He put his head on his hands and remained a moment, as if full of a silent convulsion of thought. Then he lifted his head and said in a dull voice:

"Very well. I must tell the secret."

His eyes rolled darkly over the whole darkling scene, from the red eyes of the little stove to the stark expanse of the ancient wall, over which were standing out, more and more brightly, the strong stars of the south.

"The secret is," he said; and then stopped as if unable to go on. Then he began again and said:

"You see, it was I who killed all those people."

"What?" repeated the other, in a small voice out of a vast silence.

4

"You see, I had murdered them all myself," explained Father Brown patiently. "So, of course, I knew how it was done."

Grandison Chace had risen to his great height like a man lifted to the ceiling by a sort of slow explosion. Staring down at the other he repeated his incredulous question.

"I had planned out each of the crimes very carefully," went on Father Brown, "I had thought out exactly how a thing like that could be done, and in what style or state of mind a man could really do it. And when I was quite sure that I felt exactly like the murderer myself, of course I knew who he was."

Chace gradually released a sort of broken sigh.

"You frightened me all right," he said. "For the minute I really did think you meant you were the murderer. Just for the minute I kind of saw it splashed over all the papers in the States: "Saintly Sleuth Exposed as Killer: Hundred Crimes of Father Brown.' Why, of course, if it's just a figure of speech and means you tried to reconstruct the psychogy — "

Father Brown rapped sharply on the stove with the short pipe he was about to fill; one or his very rare spasms of annoyance contracted his face.

"No, no, no," he said, almost angrily; "I don't mean just a figure of speech. This is what comes of trying to talk about deep things. . . . What's the good of words . . .? If you try to talk about a truth that's merely moral, people always think it's merely metaphorical. A real live man with two legs once said to me: 'I only believe in the Holy Ghost in a spiritual sense.' Naturally, I said: 'In what other sense could you believe it?' And then he thought I meant he needn't believe in anything except evolution, or ethical fellowship, or some bilge. . . . I mean that I really did see myself, and my real self, committing the murders. I didn't actually kill the men by material means; but that's not the point. Any brick or bit of machinery might have killed them by material means. I mean that I thought and thought about how a man might come to be like that, until I realized that I really was like that, in everything except actual final consent to the action. It was once suggested to me by a friend of mine, as a sort of religious exercise. I believe he got it from Pope Leo XIII, who was always rather a hero of mine."

"I'm afraid," said the American, in tones that were still doubtful, and keeping his eye on the priest rather as if he were a wild animal, "that you'd have to explain a lot to me before I knew what you were talking about. The science of detection — — "

Father Brown snapped his fingers with the same animated annoyance. "That's it," he cried; "that's just where we part company. Science is a grand thing when you can get it; in its real sense one of the grandest words in the world. But what do these men mean, nine times out often, when they use it nowadays? When they say detection is a science? When they say criminology is a science? They mean getting outside a man and studying him as if he were a gigantic insect: in what they would call a dry impartial light, in what I should call a dead and dehumanized light. They mean getting a long way off him, as if he were a distant prehistoric monster; staring at the shape of his 'criminal skull' as if it were a sort of eerie growth, like the horn on a rhinoceros's nose. When the scientist talks about a type, he never means himself, but always his neighbour; probably his poorer neighbour. I don't deny the dry light may sometimes do good; though in one sense it's the very reverse of science. So far from being knowledge, it's actually suppression of what we know. It's treating a friend as a stranger, and pretending that something familiar is really remote and mysterious. It's like saying that a man has a proboscis between the eyes, or that he falls down in a fit of insensibility once every twenty-four hours. Well, what you call 'the secret' is exactly the opposite. I don't try to get outside the man. I try to get inside the murderer. . . . Indeed it's much more than that, don't you see? I am inside a man. I am always inside a man, moving his arms and legs; but I wait till I know I am inside a murderer, thinking his thoughts, wrestling with his passions; till I have bent myself into the posture of his hunched and peering hatred; till I see the world with his bloodshot and squinting eyes, looking between the blinkers of his half-witted concentration; looking up the short and sharp perspective of a straight road to a pool of blood. Till I am really a murderer."

"Oh," said Mr. Chace, regarding him with a long, grim face, and added: "And that is what you call a religious exercise."

"Yes," said Father Brown; "that is what I call a religious exercise."

After an instant's silence he resumed: "It's so real a religious exercise that I'd rather not have said anything about it. But I simply couldn't have you going off and telling all your countrymen that I had a secret magic connected with Thought-Forms, could I? I've put it badly, but it's true. No man's really any good till he knows how bad he is, or might be; till he's realized exactly how much right he has to all this snobbery, and sneering, and talking about 'criminals,' as if they were apes in a forest ten thousand miles away; till he's got rid of all the dirty self-deception of talking about low types and deficient skulls; till he's squeezed out of his soul the last drop of the oil of the Pharisees; till his only hope is somehow or other to have captured one criminal, and kept him safe and sane under his own hat."

Flambeau came forward and filled a great goblet with Spanish wine and set it before his friend, as he had already set one before his fellow guest. Then he himself spoke for the first time:

"I believe Father Brown has had a new batch of mysteries. We were talking about them the other day, I fancy. He has been dealing with some queer people since we last met."

"Yes; I know the stories more or less — but not the application," said Chace, lifting his glass thoughtfully. "Can you give me any examples, I wonder. ... I mean, did you deal with this last batch in that introspective style?"

Father Brown also lifted his glass, and the glow of the fire turned the red wine transparent, like the glorious blood-red glass of a martyr's window. The red flame seemed to hold his eyes and absorb his gaze that sank deeper and deeper into it, as if that single cup held a red sea of the blood of all men, and his soul were a diver, ever plunging in dark humility and inverted imagination, lower than its lowest monsters and its most ancient slime. In that cup, as in a red mirror, he saw many things; the doings of his last days moved in crimson shadows; the examples that his companions demanded danced in symbolic shapes; and there passed before him all the stories that are told here. Now, the luminous wine was like a vast red sunset upon dark red sands, where stood dark figures of men; one was fallen and another running towards him. Then the sunset seemed to break up into patches: red lanterns swinging from garden trees and a pond gleaming red with reflection; and then all the colour seemed to cluster again into a great rose of red crystal, a jewel that irradiated the world like a red sun, save for the shadow of a tall figure with a high head-dress as of some prehistoric priest; and then faded again till nothing was left but a flame of wild red beard blowing in the wind upon a wild grey moor. All these things, which may be seen later from other angles and in other moods than his own, rose up in his memory at the challenge and began to form themselves into anecdotes and arguments.

"Yes," he said, as he raised the wine cup slowly to his lips, "I can remember pretty well — —"

II: THE MIRROR OF THE MAGISTRATE

JAMES BAGSHAW and Wilfred Underhill were old friends, and were fond of rambling through the streets at night, talking interminably as they turned corner after corner in the silent and seemingly lifeless labyrinth of the large suburb in which they lived. The former, a big, dark, good-humoured man with a strip of black moustache, was a professional police detective; the latter, a sharp-faced, sensitive- looking gentleman with light hair, was an amateur interested in detection. It will come as a shock to the readers of the best scientific romance to learn that it was the policeman who was talking and the amateur who was listening, even with a certain respect.

"Ours is the only trade," said Bagshaw, "in which the professional is always supposed to be wrong. After all, people don't write stories in which hairdressers can't cut hair and have to be helped by a customer; or in which a cabman can't drive a cab until his fare explains to him the philosophy of cab-driving. For all that, I'd never deny that we often tend to get into a rut: or, in other words, have the disadvantages of going by a rule. Where the romancers are wrong is, that they don't allow us even the advantages of going by a rule."

"Surely," said Underhill, "Sherlock Holmes would say that he went by a logical rule."

"He may be right," answered the other; "but I mean a collective rule. It's like the staff work of an army. We pool our information."

"And you don't think detective stories allow for that?" asked his friend.

"Well, let's take any imaginary case of Sherlock Holmes, and Lestrade, the official detective. Sherlock Holmes, let us say, can guess that a total stranger crossing the street is a foreigner, merely because he seems to look for the traffic to go to the right instead of the left. I'm quite ready to admit Holmes might guess that. I'm quite sure Lestrade wouldn't guess anything of the kind. But what they leave out is the fact that the policeman, who couldn't guess, might very probably know. Lestrade might know the man was a foreigner merely because his department has to keep an eye on all foreigners; some would say on all natives, too. As a policeman I'm glad the police know so much; for every man wants to do his own job well. But as a citizen, I sometimes wonder whether they don't know too much."

"You don't seriously mean to say," cried Underhill incredulously, "that you know anything about strange people in a strange street. That if a man walked out of that house over there, you would know anything about him?"

"I should if he was the householder," answered Bagshaw. "That house is rented by a literary man of Anglo-Roumanian extraction, who generally lives in Paris, but is over here in connexion with some poetical play of his. His name's Osric Orm, one of the new poets, and pretty steep to read, I believe."

"But I mean all the people down the road," said his companion. "I was thinking how strange and new and nameless everything looks, with these high blank walls and these houses lost in large gardens. You can't know all of them."

"I know a few," answered Bagshaw. "This garden wall we're walking under is at the end of the grounds of Sir Humphrey Gwynne, better known as Mr. Justice Gwynne, the old judge who made such a row about spying during the war. The house next door to it belongs to a wealthy cigar merchant. He comes from Spanish-America and looks very swarthy and Spanish himself; but he bears the very English name of Buller. The house beyond that — did you hear that noise?"

"I heard something," said Underhill, "but I really don't know what it was."

"I know what it was," replied the detective, "it was a rather heavy revolver, fired twice, followed by a cry for help. And it came straight out of the back garden of Mr. Justice Gwynne, that paradise of peace and legality."

He looked up and down the street sharply and then added:

"And the only gate of the back garden is half a mile round on the other side. I wish this wall were a little lower, or I were a little lighter; but it's got to be tried."

"It is lower a little farther on," said Underhill, "and there seems to be a tree that looks helpful."

They moved hastily along and found a place where the wall seemed to stoop abruptly, almost as if it had half-sunk into the earth; and a garden tree, flamboyant with the gayest garden blossom, straggled out of the dark enclosure and was gilded by the gleam of a solitary street- lamp. Bagshaw

10

caught the crooked branch and threw one leg over the low wall; and the next moment they stood knee-deep amid the snapping plants of a garden border.

The garden of Mr. Justice Gwynne by night was rather a singular spectacle. It was large and lay on the empty edge of the suburb, in the shadow of a tall, dark house that was the last in its line of houses. The house was literally dark, being shuttered and unlighted, at least on the side overlooking the garden. But the garden itself, which lay in its shadow: and should have been a tract of absolute darkness, showed a random glitter, like that of fading fireworks; as if a giant rocket had fallen in fire among the trees. As they advanced they were able to locate it as the light of several coloured lamps, entangled in the trees like the jewel fruits of Aladdin, and especially as the light from a small, round lake or pond, which gleamed, with pale colours as if a lamp were kindled under it.

"Is he having a party?" asked Underhill. "The garden seems to be illuminated."

"No," answered Bagshaw. "It's a hobby of his, and I believe he prefers to do it when he's alone. He likes playing with a little plant of electricity that he works from that bungalow or hut over there, where he does his work and keeps his papers. Buller, who knows him very well, says the coloured lamps are rather more often a sign he's not to be disturbed."

"Sort of red danger signals," suggested the other.

"Good Lord! I'm afraid they are danger signals!" and he began suddenly to run.

A moment after Underhill saw what he had seen. The opalescent ring of light, like the halo of the moon, round the sloping sides of the pond, was broken by two black stripes or streaks which soon proved themselves to be the long, black legs of a figure fallen head downwards into the hollow, with the head in the pond.

"Come on," cried the detective sharply, "that looks to me like — — "

His voice was lost, as he ran on across the wide lawn, faintly luminous in the artificial light, making a bee-line across the big garden for the pool and the fallen figure. Underhill was trotting steadily in that straight track, when something happened that startled him for the moment. Bagshaw, who was travelling as steadily as a bullet towards the black figure by the luminous pool, suddenly turned at a sharp angle and began to run even more rapidly towards the shadow of the house. Underhill could not imagine what he meant by the altered direction. The next moment, when the detective had vanished into the shadow of the house, there came out of that obscurity the sound of a scuffle and a curse; and Bagshaw returned lugging with him a little struggling man with red hair. The captive had evidently been escaping under the shelter of the building, when the quicker ears of the detective had heard him rustling like a bird among the bushes.

"Underhill," said the detective, "I wish you'd run on and see what's up by the pool. And now, who are you?" he asked, coming to a halt. "What's your name?"

"Michael Flood," said the stranger in a snappy fashion. He was an unnaturally lean little man, with a hooked nose too large for his face, which was colourless, like parchment, in contrast with the ginger colour of his hair. "I've got nothing to do with this. I found him lying dead and I was scared; but I only came to interview him for a paper."

"When you interview celebrities for the Press," said Bagshaw, "do you generally climb over the garden wall?"

And he pointed grimly to a trail of footprints coming and going along the path towards the flower bed.

The man calling himself Flood wore an expression equally grim.

"An interviewer might very well get over the wall," he said, "for I couldn't make anybody hear at the front door. The servant had gone out."

"How do you know he'd gone out?" asked the detective suspiciously.

"Because," said Flood, with an almost unnatural calm, "I'm not the only person who gets over garden walls. It seems just possible that you did it yourself. But, anyhow, the servant did; for I've just this moment seen him drop over the wall, away on the other side of the garden, just by the garden door."

"Then why didn't he use the garden door?" demanded the cross-examiner.

"How should I know?" retorted Flood. "Because it was shut, I suppose. But you'd better ask him, not me; he's coming towards the house at this minute."

There was, indeed, another shadowy figure beginning to be visible through the fire-shot gloaming, a squat, square-headed figure, wearing a red waistcoat as the most conspicuous part of a rather shabby livery. He appeared to be making with unobtrusive haste towards a side- door in the house, until Bagshaw halloed to him to halt. He drew nearer to them very reluctantly, revealing a heavy, yellow face, with a touch of something Asiatic which was consonant with his flat, blue-black hair.

Bagshaw turned abruptly to the man called Flood. "Is there anybody in this place," he said, "who can testify to your identity?"

"Not many, even in this country," growled Flood. "I've only just come from Ireland; the only man I know round here is the priest at St. Dominic's Church—Father Brown."

"Neither of you must leave this place," said Bagshaw, and then added to the servant: "But you can go into the house and ring up St. Dominic's Presbytery and ask Father Brown if he would mind coming round here at once. No tricks, mind."

While the energetic detective was securing the potential fugitives, his companion, at his direction, had hastened on to the actual scene of the tragedy. It was a strange enough scene; and, indeed, if the tragedy had not been tragic it would have been highly fantastic. The dead man (for the briefest examination proved him to be dead) lay with his head in the pond, where the glow of the artificial illumination encircled the head with something of the appearance of an unholy halo. The face was gaunt and rather sinister, the brow bald, and the scanty curls dark grey, like iron rings; and, despite the damage done by the bullet wound in the temple, Underhill had no difficulty in recognizing the features he had seen in the many portraits of Sir Humphrey Gwynne. The dead man was in evening-dress, and his long, black legs, so thin as to be almost spidery, were sprawling at different angles up the steep bank from which he had fallen. As by some weird whim of diabolical arabesque, blood was eddying out, very slowly, into the luminous water in snaky rings, like the transparent crimson of sunset clouds.

Underhill did not know how long he stood staring down at this macabre figure, when he looked up and saw a group of four figures standing above him on the bank. He was prepared for Bagshaw and his Irish captive, and he had no difficulty in guessing the status of the servant in the red waistcoat. But the fourth figure had a sort of grotesque solemnity that seemed strangely congruous to that incongruity. It was a stumpy figure with a round face and a hat like a black halo. He realized that it was, in fact, a priest; but there was something about it that reminded him of some quaint old black woodcut at the end of a Dance of Death.

Then he heard Bagshaw saying to the priest:

"I'm glad you can identify this man; but you must realize that he's to some extent under suspicion. Of course, he may be innocent; but he did enter the garden in an irregular fashion."

"Well, I think he's innocent myself," said the little priest in a colourless voice. "But, of course, I may be wrong."

"Why do you think he is innocent?"

"Because he entered the garden in an irregular fashion," answered the cleric. "You see, I entered it in a regular fashion myself. But I seem to be almost the only person who did. All the best people seem to get over garden walls nowadays."

"What do you mean by a regular fashion?" asked the detective.

"Well," said Father Brown, looking at him with limpid gravity, "I came in by the front door. I often come into houses that way."

"Excuse me," said Bagshaw, "but does it matter very much how you came in, unless you propose to confess to the murder?"

"Yes, I think it does," said the priest mildly. "The truth is, that when I came in at the front door I saw something I don't think any of the rest of you have seen. It seems to me it might have something to do with it."

"What did you see?"

"I saw a sort of general smash-up," said Father Brown in his mild voice. "A big looking-glass broken, and a small palm tree knocked over, and the pot smashed all over the floor. Somehow, it looked to me as if something had happened."

"You are right," said Bagshaw after a pause. "If you saw that, it certainly looks as if it had something to do with it."

"And if it had anything to do with it," said the priest very gently, "it looks as if there was one person who had nothing to do with it; and that is Mr. Michael Flood, who entered the garden over the wall in an irregular fashion, and then tried to leave it in the same irregular fashion. It is his irregularity that makes me believe in his innocence."

"Let us go into the house," said Bagshaw abruptly.

As they passed in at the side-door, the servant leading the way, Bagshaw fell back a pace or two and spoke to his friend.

"Something odd about that servant," he said. "Says his name is Green, though he doesn't look it; but there seems no doubt he's really Gwynne's servant, apparently the only regular servant he had. But the queer thing is, that he flatly denied that his master was in the garden at all, dead or alive. Said the old judge had gone out to a grand legal dinner and couldn't be home for hours, and gave that as his excuse for slipping out."

"Did he," asked Underhill, "give any excuse for his curious way of slipping in?"

'No, none that I can make sense of," answered the detective. "I can't make him out. He seems to be scared of something."

Entering by the side-door, they found themselves at the inner end of the entrance hall, which ran along the side of the house and ended with the front door, surmounted by a dreary fanlight of the old-fashioned pattern. A faint, grey light was beginning to outline its radiation upon the darkness, like some dismal and discoloured sunrise; but what light there was in the hall came from a single, shaded lamp, also of an antiquated sort, that stood on a bracket in a corner. By the light of this Bagshaw could distinguish the debris of which Brown had spoken. A tall palm, with long sweeping leaves, had fallen full length, and its dark red pot was shattered into shards. They lay littered on the carpet, along with pale and gleaming fragments of a broken mirror, of which the almost empty frame hung behind them on the wall at the end of the vestibule. At right angles to this entrance, and directly opposite the side-door as they entered, was another and similar passage leading into the rest of the house. At the other end of it could be seen the telephone which the servant had used to summon the priest; and a half- open door, showing, even through the crack, the serried ranks of great leather-bound books, marked the entrance to the judge's study.

Bagshaw stood looking down at the fallen pot and the mingled fragments at his feet.

"You're quite right," he said to the priest; "there's been a struggle here. And it must have been a struggle between Gwynne and his murderer."

"It seemed to me," said Father Brown modestly, "that something had happened here."

"Yes; it's pretty clear what happened," assented the detective. "The murderer entered by the front door and found Gwynne; probably Gwynne let him in. There was a death grapple, possibly a chance shot, that hit the glass, though they might have broken it with a stray kick or anything. Gwynne managed to free himself and fled into the garden, where he was pursued and shot finally by the pond. I fancy that's the whole story of the crime itself; but, of course, I must look round the other rooms."

The other rooms, however, revealed very little, though Bagshaw pointed significantly to the loaded automatic pistol that he found in a drawer of the library desk.

"Looks as if he was expecting this," he said; "yet it seems queer he didn't take it with him when he went out into the hall."

Eventually they returned to the hall, making their way towards the front door. Father Brown letting his eye rove around in a rather absent-minded fashion. The two corridors, monotonously papered in the same grey and faded pattern, seemed to emphasize the dust and dingy floridity of the few early Victorian ornaments, the green rust that devoured the bronze of the lamp, the dull gold that glimmered in the frame of the broken mirror.

"They say it's bad luck to break a looking-glass," he said. "This looks like the very house of ill-luck. There's something about the very furniture?

"

"That's rather odd," said Bagshaw sharply. "I thought the front door would be shut, but it's left on the latch."

There was no reply; and they passed out of the front door into the front garden, a narrower and more formal plot of flowers, having at one end a curiously clipped hedge with a hole in it, like a green cave, under the shadow of which some broken steps peeped out.

Father Brown strolled up to the hole and ducked his head under it. A few moments after he had disappeared they were astonished to hear his quiet voice in conversation above their heads, as if he were talking to somebody at the top of a tree. The detective followed, and found that the curious covered stairway led to what looked like a broken bridge, over-hanging the darker and emptier spaces of the garden. It just curled round the corner of the house, bringing in sight the field of coloured lights beyond and beneath. Probably it was the relic of some abandoned

16

architectural fancy of building a sort of terrace on arches across the lawn. Bagshaw thought it a curious cul-de-sac in which to find anybody in the small hours between night and morning; but he was not looking at the details of it just then. He was looking at the man who was found.

As the man stood with his back turned — a small man in light grey clothes — the one outstanding feature about him was a wonderful head of hair, as yellow and radiant as the head of a huge dandelion. It was literally outstanding like a halo, and something in that association made the face, when it was slowly and sulkily turned on them, rather a shock of contrast. That halo should have enclosed an oval face of the mildly angelic sort; but the face was crabbed and elderly with a powerful jowl and a short nose that somehow suggested the broken nose of a pugilist.

"This is Mr. Orm, the celebrated poet, I understand," said Father Brown, as calmly as if he were introducing two people in a drawing-room.

"Whoever he is," said Bagshaw, "I must trouble him to come with me and answer a few questions."

Mr. Osric Orm, the poet, was not a model of self-expression when it came to the answering of questions. There, in that corner of the old garden, as the grey twilight before dawn began to creep over the heavy hedges and the broken bridge, and afterwards in a succession of circumstances and stages of legal inquiry that grew more and more ominous, he refused to say anything except that he had intended to call on Sir Humphrey Gwynne, but had not done so because he could not get anyone to answer the bell. When it was pointed out that the door was practically open, he snorted. When it was hinted that the hour was somewhat late, he snarled. The little that he said was obscure, either because he really knew hardly any English, or because he knew better than to know any. His opinions seemed to be of a nihilistic and destructive sort, as was indeed the tendency of his poetry for those who could follow it; and it seemed possible that his business with the judge, and perhaps his quarrel with the judge, had been something in the anarchist line. Gwynne was known to have had something of a mania about Bolshevist spies, as he had about German spies. Anyhow, one coincidence, only a few moments after his capture, confirmed Bagshaw in the impression that the case must be taken seriously. As they went out of the front gate into the street, they so happened to encounter yet another neighbour, Duller, the cigar merchant from next door, conspicuous by his brown, shrewd face and the unique orchid in his buttonhole; for he had a name in that branch of horticulture. Rather to the surprise of the rest, he hailed his neighbour, the poet, in a matter -of-fact manner, almost as if he had expected to see him. "Hallo, here we are again," he said. "Had a long talk with old Gwynne, I suppose?"

"Sir Humphrey Gwynne is dead," said Bagshaw. "I am investigating the case and I must ask you to explain."

Buller stood as still as the lamp-post beside him, possibly stiffened with surprise. The red end of his cigar brightened and darkened rhythmically, but his brown face was in shadow; when he spoke it was with quite a new voice.

"I only mean," he said, "that when I passed two hours ago Mr. Orm was going in at this gate to see Sir Humphrey."

"He says he hasn't seen him yet," observed Bagshaw, "or even been into the house."

"It's a long time to stand on the door-step," observed Buller.

"Yes," said Father Brown; "it's rather a long time to stand in the street."

"I've been home since then," said the cigar merchant. "Been writing letters and came out again to post them."

"You'll have to tell all that later," said Bagshaw. "Good night — or good morning."

The trial of Osric Orm for the murder of Sir Humphrey Gwynne, which filled the newspapers for so many weeks, really turned entirely on the same crux as that little talk under the lamp-post, when the grey- green dawn was breaking about the dark streets and gardens. Everything came back to the enigma of those two empty hours between the time when Buller saw Orm going in at the garden gate, and the time when Father Brown found him apparently still lingering in the garden. He had certainly had the time to commit six murders, and might almost have committed them for want of something to do; for he could give no coherent account of what he was doing. It was argued by the prosecution that he had also the opportunity, as the front door was unlatched, and the side-door into the larger garden left standing open. The court followed, with considerable interest, Bagshaw's clear reconstruction of the struggle in the passage, of which the traces were so evident; indeed, the police had since found the shot that had shattered the glass. Finally, the hole in the hedge to which he had been tracked, had very much the appearance of a hiding-place. On the other hand. Sir Matthew Blake, the very able counsel for the defence, turned this last argument the other way: asking why any man should entrap himself in a place without possible exit, when it would obviously be much more sensible to slip out into the street. Sir Matthew Blake also made effective use of the mystery that still rested upon the motive for the murder. Indeed, upon this point, the passages between Sir Matthew Blake and Sir Arthur Travers, the equally brilliant advocate for the prosecution, turned rather to the advantage of the prisoner. Sir Arthur could only throw out suggestions about a Bolshevist conspiracy which sounded a little thin. But when it came to investigating the facts of Orm's mysterious behaviour that night he was considerably more effective.

The prisoner went into the witness-box, chiefly because his astute counsel calculated that it would create a bad impression if he did not. But he was almost as uncommunicative to his own counsel as to the prosecuting counsel. Sir Arthur Travers made all possible capital out of his stubborn silence, but did not succeed in breaking it. Sir Arthur was a long, gaunt man, with a long, cadaverous face, in striking contrast to the sturdy figure and bright, bird-like eye of Sir Matthew Blake. But if Sir Matthew suggested a very cocksure sort of cock sparrow, Sir Arthur might more truly have been compared to a crane or stork; as he leaned forward, prodding the poet with questions, his long nose might have been a long beak.

"Do you mean to tell the jury," he asked, in tones of grating incredulity, "that you never went in to see the deceased gentleman at all?"

"No!" replied Orm shortly.

"You wanted to see him, I suppose. You must have been very anxious to see him. Didn't you wait two whole hours in front of his front door?"

"Yes," replied the other.

"And yet you never even noticed the door was open?"

"No," said Orm.

"What in the world were you doing for two hours in somebody else's front garden?" insisted the barrister; "You were doing something, I suppose?"

"Yes."

"Is it a secret?" asked Sir Arthur, with adamantine jocularity.

"It's a secret from you," answered the poet.

It was upon this suggestion of a secret that Sir Arthur seized in developing his line of accusation. With a boldness which some thought unscrupulous, he turned the very mystery of the motive, which was the strongest part of his opponent's case, into an argument for his own. He gave it as the first fragmentary hint of some far-flung and elaborate conspiracy, in which a patriot had perished like one caught in the coils of an octopus.

"Yes," he cried in a vibrating voice, "my learned friend is perfectly right! We do not know the exact reason why this honourable public servant was murdered. We shall not know the reason why the next public servant is murdered. If my learned friend himself falls a victim to his eminence, and the hatred which the hellish powers of destruction feel for the guardians of law, he will be murdered, and he will not know the reason. Half the decent people in this court will be butchered in their beds, and we shall not know the reason. And we shall never know the reason and never arrest the massacre, until it has depopulated our country, so long as the defence is permitted to stop all proceedings with this stale tag about 'motive,' when every other fact in the case, every glaring incongruity, every gaping silence, tells us that we stand in the presence of Cain."

"I never knew Sir Arthur so excited," said Bagshaw to his group of companions afterwards. "Some people are saying he went beyond the usual limit and that the prosecutor in a murder case oughtn't to be so vindictive. But I must say there was something downright creepy about that little goblin with the yellow hair that seemed to play up to the impression. I was vaguely recalling, all the time, something that De Quincey says about Mr. Williams, that ghastly criminal who slaughtered two whole families almost in silence. I think he says that Williams had hair of a vivid unnatural yellow; and that he thought it had been dyed by a trick learned in India, where they dye horses green or blue. Then there was his queer, stony silence, like a troglodyte's; I'll never deny that it all worked me up until I felt there was a sort of monster in the dock. If that was only Sir Arthur's eloquence, then he certainly took a heavy responsibility in putting so much passion into it."

"He was a friend of poor Gwynne's, as a matter of fact," said Underhill, more gently; "a man I know saw them hobnobbing together after a great legal dinner lately. I dare say that's why he feels so strongly in this case. I suppose it's doubtful whether a man ought to act in such a case on mere personal feeling."

"He wouldn't," said Bagshaw. "I bet Sir Arthur Travers wouldn't act only on feeling, however strongly he felt. He's got a very stiff sense of his own professional position. He's one of those men who are ambitious even when they've satisfied their ambition. I know nobody who'd take more trouble to keep his position in the world. No; you've got hold of the wrong moral to his rather thundering sermon. If he lets himself go like that, it's because he thinks he can get a conviction, anyhow, and wants to put himself at the head of some political movement against the conspiracy he talks about. He must have some very good reason for wanting to convict Orm and some very good reason for thinking he can do it. That means that the facts will support him. His confidence doesn't look well for the prisoner." He became conscious of an insignificant figure in the group.

"Well, Father Brown," he said with a smile; "what do you think of our judicial procedure?"

"Well," replied the priest rather absently, "I think the thing that struck me most was how different men look in their wigs. You talk about the prosecuting barrister being so tremendous. But I happened to see him take his wig off for a minute, and he really looks quite a different man. He's quite bald, for one thing."

"I'm afraid that won't prevent his being tremendous," answered Bagshaw. "You don't propose to found the defence on the fact that the prosecuting counsel is bald, do you?"

"Not exactly," said Father Brown good-humouredly. "To tell the truth, I was thinking how little some kinds of people know about other kinds of people. Suppose I went among some remote people who had never even heard of England. Suppose I told them that there is a man in my country who won't ask a question of life and death, until he has put an erection made of horse-hair on the top of his head, with little tails behind, and grey corkscrew curls at the side, like an Early Victorian old woman. They would think he must be rather eccentric; but he isn't at all eccentric, he's only conventional. They would think so, because they don't know anything

21

about English barristers; because they don't know what a barrister is. Well, that barrister doesn't know what a poet is. He doesn't understand that a poet's eccentricities wouldn't seem eccentric to other poets. He thinks it odd that Orm should walk about in a beautiful garden for two hours, with nothing to do. God bless my soul! A poet would think nothing of walking about in the same backyard for ten hours if he had a poem to do. Orm's own counsel was quite as stupid. It never occurred to him to ask Orm the obvious question."

"What question do you mean?" asked the other.

"Why, what poem he was making up, of course," said Father Brown rather impatiently. "What line he was stuck at, what epithet he was looking for, what climax he was trying to work up to. If there were any educated people in court, who know what literature is, they would have known well enough whether he had had anything genuine to do. You'd have asked a manufacturer about the conditions of his factory; but nobody seems to consider the conditions under which poetry is manufactured. It's done by doing nothing."

"That's all very well," replied the detective; "but why did he hide? Why did he climb up that crooked little stairway and stop there; it led nowhere."

"Why, because it led nowhere, of course," cried Father Brown explosively. "Anybody who clapped eyes on that blind alley ending in mid -air might have known an artist would want to go there, just as a child would."

He stood blinking for a moment, and then said apologetically: "I beg your pardon; but it seems odd that none of them understand these things. And then there was another thing. Don't you know that everything has, for an artist, one aspect or angle that is exactly right? A tree, a cow, and a cloud, in a certain relation only, mean something; as three letters, in one order only, mean a word. Well, the view of that illuminated garden from that unfinished bridge was the right view of it. It was as unique as the fourth dimension. It was a sort of fairy foreshortening; it was like looking down at heaven and seeing all the stars growing on trees and that luminous pond like a moon fallen flat on the fields in some happy nursery talc. He could have looked at it for ever. If you told him the path led nowhere, he would tell you it had led him to the country at the end of the world. But do you expect him to tell you that in the witness box? What would you say to him if he did? You talk about a man having a jury of his peers. Why don't you have a jury of poets?"

"You talk as if you were a poet yourself," said Bagshaw.

"Thank your stars I'm not," said Father Brown. "Thank your lucky stars a priest has to be more charitable than a poet. Lord have mercy on us, if you knew what a crushing, what a cruel contempt he feels for the lot of you, you'd feel as if you were under Niagara."

"You may know more about the artistic temperament than I do," said Bagshaw after a pause; "but, after all, the answer is simple. You can only show that he might have done what he did, without committing the crime. But it's equally true that he might have committed the crime. And who else could have committed it?"

"Have you thought about the servant, Green?" asked Father Brown, reflectively. "He told a rather queer story."

"Ah," cried Bagshaw quickly, "you think Green did it, after all."

"I'm quite sure he didn't," replied the other. "I only asked if you'd thought about his queer story. He only went out for some trifle, a drink or an assignation or what not. But he went out by the garden door and came back over the garden wall. In other words, he left the door open, but he came back to find it shut. Why? Because Somebody Else had already passed out that way."

"The murderer," muttered the detective doubtfully. "Do you know who he was?"

"I know what he looked like," answered Father Brown quietly. "That's the only thing I do know. I can almost see him as he came in at the front door, in the gleam of the hall lamp; his figure, his clothes, even his face!"

"What's all this?"

"He looked like Sir Humphrey Gwynne," said the priest.

"What the devil do you mean?" demanded Bagshaw. "Gwynne was lying dead with his head in the pond."

"Oh, yes," said Father Brown.

After a moment he went on: "Let's go back to that theory of yours, which was a very good one, though I don't quite agree with it. You suppose the murderer came in at the front door, met the Judge in the front hall, struggling with him and breaking the mirror; that the judge then retreated into the garden, where he was finally shot. Somehow, it doesn't sound natural to me. Granted he retreated down the hall, there are two exits at the end, one into the garden and one into the house. Surely, he would be more likely to retreat into the house? His gun was there; his telephone was there; his servant, so far as he knew, was there. Even the nearest neighbours were in that direction. Why should he stop to open the garden door and go out alone on the deserted side of the house?"

"But we know he did go out of the house," replied his companion, puzzled. "We know he went out of the house, because he was found in the garden."

"He never went out of the house, because he never was in the house," said Father Brown. "Not that evening, I mean. He was sitting in that bungalow. I read that lesson in the dark, at the beginning, in red and golden stars across the garden. They were worked from the hut; they wouldn't have been burning at all if he hadn't been in the hut. He was trying to run across to the house and the telephone, when the murderer shot him beside the pond."

"But what about the pot and the palm and the broken mirror?" cried Bagshaw. "Why, it was you who found them! It was you yourself who said there must have been a struggle in the hall."

The priest blinked rather painfully. "Did I?" he muttered. "Surely, I didn't say that. I never thought that. What I think I said, was that something had happened in the hall. And something did happen; but it wasn't a struggle."

"Then what broke the mirror?" asked Bagshaw shortly.

"A bullet broke the mirror," answered Father Brown gravely; "a bullet fired by the criminal. The big fragments of falling glass were quite enough to knock over the pot and the palm."

"Well, what else could he have been firing at except Gwynne?" asked the detective.

"It's rather a fine metaphysical point," answered his clerical companion almost dreamily. "In one sense, of course, he was firing at Gwynne. But Gwynne wasn't there to be fired at. The criminal was alone in the hall."

He was silent for a moment, and then went on quietly. "Imagine the looking-glass at the end of the passage, before it was broken, and the tall palm arching over it. In the half-light, reflecting these monochrome walls, it would, look like the end of the passage. A man reflected in it would look like a man coming from inside the house. It would look like the master of the house — if only the reflection were a little like him."

"Stop a minute," cried Bagshaw. "I believe I begin — — "

"You begin to see," said Father Brown. "You begin to see why all the suspects in this case must be innocent. Not one of them could possibly have mistaken his own reflection for old Gwynne. Orm would have known at once that his bush of yellow hair was not a bald head. Flood would have seen his own red head, and Green his own red waistcoat. Besides, they're all short and shabby; none of them could have thought his own image was a tall, thin, old gentleman in evening-dress. We want another, equally tall and thin, to match him. That's what I meant by saying that I knew what the murderer looked like."

"And what do you argue from that?" asked Bagshaw, looking at him steadily.

The priest uttered a sort of sharp, crisp laugh, oddly different from his ordinary mild manner of speech.

"I am going to argue," he said, "the very thing that you said was so ludicrous and impossible."

"What do you mean?"

"I'm going to base the defence," said Father Brown, "on the fact that the prosecuting counsel has a bald head."

"Oh, my God!" said the detective quietly, and got to his feet, staring.

Father Brown had resumed his monologue in an unruffled manner.

"You've been following the movements of a good many people in this business; you policemen were prodigiously interested in the movements of the poet, and the servant, and the Irishman. The man whose movements seem to have been rather forgotten is the dead man himself. His servant was quite honestly astonished at finding his master had returned. His master had gone to a great dinner of all the leaders of the legal profession, but had left it abruptly and come home. He was not ill, for he summoned no assistance; he had almost certainly quarrelled with some leader of the legal profession. It's among the leaders of that profession that we should have looked first for his enemy. He returned, and shut himself up in the bungalow, where he kept all his private documents about treasonable practices. But the leader of the legal profession, who knew there was something against him in those documents, was thoughtful enough to follow his accuser home; he also being in evening-dress, but with a pistol in his pocket. That is all; and nobody could ever have guessed it except for the mirror."

He seemed to be gazing into vacancy for a moment, and then added:

"A queer thing is a mirror; a picture frame that holds hundreds of different pictures, all vivid and all vanished for ever. Yet, there was something specially strange about the glass that hung at the end of that grey corridor under that green palm. It is as if it was a magic glass and had a different fate from others, as if its picture could somehow survive it, hanging in the air of that twilight house like a spectre; or at least like an abstract diagram, the skeleton of an argument. We could, at least, conjure out of the void the thing that Sir Arthur Travers saw. And by the way, there was one very true thing that you said about him."

"I'm glad to hear it," said Bagshaw with grim good nature. "What was it?"

"You said," observed the priest, "that Sir Arthur must have some good reason for wanting to get Orm hanged."

A week later the priest met the police detective once more, and learned that the authorities had already been moving on the new lines of inquiry when they were interrupted by a sensational event.

"Sir Arthur Travers," began Father Brown.

"Sir Arthur Travers is dead," said Bagshaw, briefly.

"Ah!" said the other, with a little catch in his voice; "you mean that he —
"

"Yes," said Bagshaw, "he shot at the same man again, but not in a mirror."

III: THE MAN WITH TWO BEARDS

THIS tale was told by Father Brown to Professor Crake, the celebrated criminologist, after dinner at a club, where the two were introduced to each other as sharing a harmless hobby of murder and robbery. But, as Father Brown's version rather minimized his own part in the matter, it is here re-told in a more impartial style. It arose out of a playful passage of arms, in which the professor was very scientific and the priest rather sceptical.

"My good sir," said the professor in remonstrance, "don't you believe that criminology is a science?"

"I'm not sure," replied Father Brown. "Do you believe that hagiology is a science?"

"What's that?" asked the specialist sharply.

"No; it's not the study of hags, and has nothing to do with burning witches," said the priest, smiling. "It's the study of holy things, saints and so on. You see, the Dark Ages tried to make a science about good people. But our own humane and enlightened age is only interested in a science about bad ones. Yet I think our general experience is that every conceivable sort of man has been a saint. And I suspect you will find, too, that every conceivable sort of man has been a murderer."

"Well, we believe murderers can be pretty well classified," observed Crake. "The list sounds rather long and dull; but I think it's exhaustive. First, all killing can be divided into rational and irrational, and we'll take the last first, because they are much fewer. There is such a thing as homicidal mania, or love of butchery in the abstract. There is such a thing as irrational antipathy, though it's very seldom homicidal. Then we come to the true motives: of these, some are less rational in the sense of being merely romantic and retrospective. Acts of pure revenge are acts of hopeless revenge. Thus a lover will sometimes kill a rival he could never supplant, or a rebel assassinate a tyrant after the conquest is complete. But, more often, even these acts have a rational explanation. They are hopeful murders. They fall into the larger section of the second division, of what we may call prudential crimes. These, again, fall chiefly under two descriptions. A man kills either in order to obtain what the other man possesses, either by theft or inheritance, or to stop the other man from acting in some way: as in the case of killing a blackmailer or a political opponent; or, in the case of a rather more passive obstacle, a husband or wife whose continued functioning, as such, interferes with other things. We believe that classification is pretty thoroughly thought out and, properly applied, covers the whole ground-But I'm afraid that it perhaps sounds rather dull; I hope I'm not boring you."

"Not at all," said Father Brown. "If I seemed a little absent-minded I must apologize; the truth is, I was thinking of a man I once knew. He was a murderer; but I can't see where he fits into your museum of murderers. He was not mad, nor did he like killing. He did not hate the man he killed; he hardly knew him, and certainly had nothing to avenge on him. The other man did not possess anything that he could possibly want. The other man was not behaving in any way which the murderer wanted to stop. The murdered man was not in a position to hurt, or hinder, or even affect the murderer in any way. There was no woman in the case. There were no politics in the case. This man killed a fellow- creature who was practically a stranger, and that for a very strange reason; which is possibly unique in human history."

And so, in his own more conversational fashion, he told the story. The story may well begin in a sufficiently respectable setting, at the breakfast table of a worthy though wealthy suburban family named Bankes, where the normal discussion of the newspaper had, for once, been silenced by the discussion about a mystery nearer home. Such people are sometimes accused of gossip about their neighbours, but they are in that matter almost inhumanly innocent. Rustic villagers tell tales about their neighbours, true and false; but the curious culture of the modern suburb will believe anything it is told in the papers about the wickedness of the Pope, or the martyrdom of the King of the Cannibal Islands, and, in the excitement of these topics, never knows what is happening next door. In this case, however, the two forms of interest actually coincided in a coincidence of thrilling intensity. Their own suburb had actually been mentioned in their favourite newspaper. It seemed to them like a new proof of their own existence when they saw the name in print. It was almost as if they had been unconscious and invisible before; and now they were as real as the King of the Cannibal Islands.

It was stated in the paper that a once famous criminal, known as Michael Moonshine, and many other names that were presumably not his own, had recently been released after a long term of imprisonment for his numerous burglaries; that his whereabouts was being kept quiet, but that he was believed to have settled down in the suburb in question, which we will call for convenience Chisham. A resume of some of his famous and daring exploits and escapes was given in the same issue. For it is a character of that kind of press, intended for that kind of public, that it assumes that its reader have no memories. While the peasant will remember an outlaw like Robin Hood or Rob Roy for centuries, the clerk will hardly remember the name of the criminal about whom he argued in trams and tubes two years before. Yet, Michael Moonshine had really shown some of the heroic rascality of Rob Roy or Robin Hood. He was worthy to be turned into legend and not merely into news. He was far too capable a burglar to be a murderer. But his terrific strength and the ease with which he knocked policemen over like ninepins, stunned people, and bound and gagged them, gave something almost like a final touch of fear or mystery to the fact that he never killed them. People almost felt that he would have been more human if he had.

Mr. Simon Bankes, the father of the family, was at once better read and more old-fashioned than the rest. He was a sturdy man, with a short grey beard and a brow barred with wrinkles. He had a turn for anecdotes and reminiscence, and he distinctly remembered the days when Londoners had lain awake listening for Mike Moonshine as they did for Spring-heeled Jack. Then there was his wife, a thin, dark lady. There was a sort of acid elegance about her, for her family had much more money than her husband's, if rather less education; and she even possessed a very valuable emerald necklace upstairs, that gave her a right to prominence in a discussion about thieves. There was his daughter. Opal, who was also thin and dark and supposed to be psychic — at any rate, by herself; for she had little domestic encouragement. Spirits of an ardently astral turn will be well advised not to materialize as members of a large family. There was her brother John, a burly youth, particularly boisterous in his indifference to her spiritual development; and otherwise distinguishable only by his interest in motor-cars. He seemed to be always in the act of selling one car and buying another; and by some process, hard for the economic theorist to follow, it was always possible to buy a much better article by selling the one that was damaged or discredited. There was his brother Philip, a young man with dark curly hair, distinguished by his attention to dress; which is doubtless part of the duty of a stockbroker's clerk, but, as the stockbroker was prone to hint, hardly the whole of it. Finally, there was present at this family scene his friend, Daniel Devine, who was also dark and exquisitely dressed, but bearded in a fashion that was somewhat foreign, and therefore, for many, slightly menacing.

It was Devine who had introduced the topic of the newspaper paragraph, tactfully insinuating so effective an instrument of distraction at what looked like the beginning of a small family quarrel; for the psychic lady had begun the description of a vision she had had of pale faces floating in empty night outside her window, and John Bankes was trying to roar down this revelation of a higher state with more than his usual heartiness.

But the newspaper reference to their new and possibly alarming neighbour soon put both controversialists out of court.

"How frightful," cried Mrs. Bankes. "He must be quite a new-comer; but who can he possibly be?"

"I don't know any particularly new-comers," said her husband, "except Sir Leopold Pulman, at Beechwood House."

"My dear," said the lady, "how absurd you are—Sir Leopold!" Then, after a pause, she added: "If anybody suggested his secretary now — that man with the whiskers; I've always said, ever since he got the place Philip ought to have had — — "

"Nothing doing," said Philip languidly, making his sole contribution to the conversation. "Not good enough."

"The only one I know," observed Devine, "is that man called Carver, who is stopping at Smith's Farm. He lives a very quiet life, but he's quite interesting to talk to. I think John has had some business with him."

"Knows a bit about cars," conceded the monomaniac John. "He'll know a bit more when he's been in my new car."

Devine smiled slightly; everybody had been threatened with the hospitality of John's new car. Then he added reflectively:

"That's a little what I feel about him. He knows a lot about motoring and travelling, and the active ways of the world, and yet he always stays at home pottering about round old Smith's beehives. Says he's only interested in bee culture, and that's why he's staying with Smith. It seems a very quiet hobby for a man of his sort. However, I've no doubt John's car will shake him up a bit."

As Devine walked away from the house that evening his dark face wore an expression of concentrated thought. His thoughts would, perhaps, have been worthy of our attention, even at this stage; but it is enough to say that their practical upshot was a resolution to pay an immediate visit to Mr. Carver at the house of Mr. Smith. As he was making his way thither he encountered Barnard, the secretary at Beechwood House, conspicuous by his lanky figure and the large side whiskers which Mrs. Bankes counted among her private wrongs. Their acquaintance was slight, and their conversation brief and casual; but Devine seemed to find in it food for further cogitation.

"Look here," he said abruptly, "excuse my asking, but is it true that Lady Pulman has some very famous jewellery up at the House? I'm not a professional thief, but I've just heard there's one hanging about."

"I'll get her to give an eye to them," answered the secretary. "To tell the truth, I've ventured to warn her about them already myself. I hope she has attended to it."

As they spoke, there came the hideous cry of a motor-horn just behind, and John Bankes came to a stop beside them, radiant at his own steering - wheel. When he heard of Devine's destination he claimed it as his own, though his tone suggested rather an abstract relish for offering people a ride. The ride was consumed in continuous praises of the car, now mostly in the matter of its adaptability to weather.

"Shuts up as tight as a box," he said, "and opens as easy — as easy as opening your mouth."

Devine's mouth, at the moment, did not seem so easy to open, and they arrived at Smith's farm to the sound of a soliloquy. Passing the outer gate, Devine found the man he was looking for without going into the house. The man was walking about in the garden, with his hands in his pockets, wearing a large, limp straw hat; a man with a long face and a large chin. The wide brim cut off the upper part of his face with a shadow that looked a little like a mask. In the background was a row of sunny beehives, along which an elderly man, presumably Mr. Smith, was moving accompanied by a short, commonplace-looking companion in black clerical costume.

"I say," burst in the irrepressible John, before Devine could offer any polite greeting, "I've brought her round to give you a little run. You see if she isn't better than a 'Thunderbolt.'"

Mr Carver's mouth set into a smile that may have been meant to be gracious, but looked rather grim. "I'm afraid I shall be too busy for pleasure this evening," he said.

"How doth the little busy bee," observed Devine, equally enigmatically. "Your bees must be very busy if they keep you at it all night. I was wondering if — — "

"Well," demanded Carver, with a certain cool defiance.

"Well, they say we should make hay while the sun shines," said Devine. "Perhaps you make honey while the moon shines."

There came a flash from the shadow of the broad-brimmed hat, as the whites of the man's eyes shifted and shone.

"Perhaps there is a good deal of moonshine in the business," he said: "but I warn you my bees do not only make honey. They sting."

"Are you coming along in the car?" insisted the staring John. But Carver, though he threw off the momentary air of sinister significance with which he had been answering Devine, was still positive in his polite refusal.

"I can't possibly go," he said. "Got a lot of writing to do. Perhaps you'd be kind enough to give some of my friends a run, if you want a companion. This is my friend, Mr. Smith, Father Brown-"

"Of course," cried Bankes; "let 'em all come."

"Thank you very much," said Father Brown. "I'm afraid I shall have to decline; I've got to go on to Benediction in a few minutes."

"Mr. Smith is your man, then," said Carver, with something almost like impatience. "I'm sure Smith is longing for a motor ride."

Smith, who wore a broad grin, bore no appearance of longing for anything. He was an active little old man with a very honest wig; one of those wigs that look no more natural than a hat. Its tinge of yellow was out of keeping with his colourless complexion. He shook his head and answered with amiable obstinacy:

"I remember I went over this road ten years ago—in one of those contraptions. Came over in it from my sister's place at Holmgate, and never been over that road in a car since. It was rough going I can tell you,"

"Ten years ago!" scoffed John Bankes. "Two thousand years ago you went in an ox wagon. Do you think cars haven't changed in ten years — and roads, too, for that matter? In my little bus you don't know the wheels are going round. You think you're just flying."

"I'm sure Smith wants to go flying," urged Carver. "It's the dream of his life. Come, Smith, go over to Holmgate and see your sister. You know you ought to go and see your sister. Go over and stay the night if you like."

"Well, I generally walk over, so I generally do stay the night," said old Smith. "No need to trouble the gentleman to-day, particularly."

"But think what fun it will be for your sister to see you arrive in a car!" cried Carver. "You really ought to go. Don't be so selfish."

"That's it," assented Bankes, with buoyant benevolence. "Don't you be selfish. It won't hurt you. You aren't afraid of it, are you?"

"Well," said Mr. Smith, blinking thoughtfully, "I don't want to be selfish, and I don't think I'm afraid-I'll come with you if you put it that way."

The pair drove off, amid waving salutations that seemed somehow to give the little group the appearance of a cheering crowd. Yet Devine and the priest only joined in out of courtesy, and they both felt it was the dominating gesture of their host that gave it its final air of farewell. The detail gave them a curious sense of the pervasive force of his personality.

The moment the car was out of sight he turned to them with a sort of boisterous apology and said: "Well!"

He said it with that curious heartiness which is the reverse of hospitality. That extreme geniality is the same as a dismissal.

"I must be going," said Devine. "We must not interrupt the busy bee. I'm afraid I know very little about bees; sometimes I can hardly tell a bee from a wasp."

"I've kept wasps, too," answered the mysterious Mr. Carver. When his guests were a few yards down the street, Devine said rather impulsively to his companion: "Rather an odd scene that, don't you think?"

"Yes," replied Father Brown. "And what do you think about it?"

Devine looked at the little man in black, and something in the gaze of his great, grey eyes seemed to renew his impulse.

33

"I think," he said, "that Carver was very anxious to have the house to himself tonight. I don't know whether you had any such suspicions?"

"I may have my suspicions," replied the priest, "but I'm not sure whether they're the same as yours."

That evening, when the last dusk was turning into dark in the gardens round the family mansion, Opal Bankes was moving through some of the dim and empty rooms with even more than her usual abstraction; and anyone who had looked at her closely would have noted that her pale face had more than its usual pallor. Despite its bourgeois luxury, the house as a whole had a rather unique shade of melancholy. It was the sort of immediate sadness that belongs to things that are old rather than ancient. It was full of faded fashions, rather than historic customs; of the order and ornament that is just recent enough to be recognized as dead. Here and there, Early Victorian coloured glass tinted the twilight; the high ceilings made the long rooms look narrow; and at the end of the long room down which she was walking was one of those round windows, to be found in the buildings of its period. As she came to about the middle of the room, she stopped, and then suddenly swayed a little, as if some invisible hand had struck her on the face.

An instant after there was the noise or knocking on the front door, dulled by the closed doors between. She knew that the rest of the household were in the upper parts of the house, but she could not have analysed the motive that made her go to the front door herself. On the doorstep stood a dumpy and dingy figure in black, which she recognized as the Roman Catholic priest, whose name was Brown. She knew him only slightly; but she liked him. He did not encourage her psychic views; quite the contrary; but he discouraged them as if they mattered and not as if they did not matter. It was not so much that he did not sympathize with her opinions, as that he did sympathize but did not agree. All this was in some sort of chaos in her mind as she found herself saying, without greeting, or waiting to hear his business:

"I'm so glad you've come. I've seen a ghost."

"There's no need to be distressed about that," he said. "It often happens. Most of the ghosts aren't ghosts, and the few that may be won't do you any harm. Was it any ghost in particular?"

"No," she admitted, with a vague feeling of relief, "it wasn't so much the thing itself as an atmosphere of awful decay, a sort of luminous ruin. It was a face. A face at the window. But it was pale and goggling, and looked like the picture of Judas."

"Well, some people do look like that," reflected the priest, "and I dare say they look in at windows, sometimes. May I come in and see where it happened?"

When she returned to the room with the visitor, however, other members of the family had assembled, and those of a less psychic habit had thought it convenient to light the lamps. In the presence of Mrs. Bankes, Father Brown assumed a more conventional civility, and apologized for his intrusion.

"I'm afraid it is taking a liberty with your house, Mrs. Bankes," he said. "But I think I can explain how the business happens to concern you. I was up at the Pulmans' place just now, when I was rung up and asked to come round here to meet a man who is coming to communicate something that may be of some moment to you. I should not have added myself to the party, only I am wanted, apparently, because I am a witness to what has happened up at Beechwood. In fact, it was I who had to give the alarm."

"What has happened?" repeated the lady.

"There has been a robbery up, at Beechwood House," said Father Brown, gravely; "a robbery, and what I fear is worse, Lady Pulman's jewels have gone; and her unfortunate secretary, Mr. Barnard, was picked up in the garden, having evidently been shot by the escaping burglar."

"That man," ejaculated the lady of the house. "I believe he was — —"

She encountered the grave gaze of the priest, and her words suddenly went from her; she never knew why.

"I communicated with the police," he went on, "and with another authority interested in this case; and they say that even a superficial examination has revealed foot-prints and finger-prints and other indications of a well-known criminal."

At this point, the conference was for a moment disturbed, by the return of John Bankes, from what appeared to be an abortive expedition in the car. Old Smith seemed to have been a disappointing passenger, after all.

"Funked it, after all, at the last minute," he announced with noisy disgust. "Bolted off while I was looking at what I thought was a puncture. Last time I'll take one of these yokels ─ ─"

But his complaints received small attention in the general excitement that gathered round Father Brown and his news.

"Somebody will arrive in a moment," went on the priest, with the same air of weighty reserve, "who will relieve me of this responsibility. When I have confronted you with him I shall have done my duty as a witness in a serious business. It only remains for me to say that a servant up at Beechwood House told me that she had seen a face at one of the windows ─ ─"

"I saw a face," said Opal, "at one of our windows."

"Oh, you are always seeing faces," said her brother John roughly.

"It is as well to see facts even if they are faces," said Father Brown equably, "and I think the face you saw ─ ─"

Another knock at the front door sounded through the house, and a minute afterwards the door of the room opened and another figure appeared. Devine half-rose from his chair at the sight of it.

It was a tall, erect figure, with a long, rather cadaverous face, ending in a formidable chin. The brow was rather bald, and the eyes bright and blue, which Devine had last seen obscured with a broad straw hat.

"Pray don't let anybody move," said the man called Carver, in clear and courteous tones. But to Devine's disturbed mind the courtesy had an ominous resemblance to that of a brigand who holds a company motionless with a pistol.

"Please sit down, Mr. Devine," said Carver; "and, with Mrs. Bankes's permission, I will follow your example. My presence here necessitates an explanation. I rather fancy you suspected me of being an eminent and distinguished burglar."

"I did," said Devine grimly.

"As you remarked," said Carver, "it is not always easy to know a wasp from a bee."

After a pause, he continued: "I can claim to be one of the more useful, though equally annoying, insects. I am a detective, and I have come down to investigate an alleged renewal of the activities of the criminal calling himself Michael Moonshine. Jewel robberies were his speciality; and there has just been one of them at Beechwood House, which, by all the technical tests, is obviously his work. Not only do the prints correspond, but you may possibly know that when he was last arrested, and it is believed on other occasions also, he wore a simple but effective disguise of a red beard and a pair of large horn-rimmed spectacles."

Opal Bankes leaned forward fiercely.

"That was it," she cried in excitement, "that was the face I saw, with great goggles and a red, ragged beard like Judas. I thought it was a ghost."

"That was also the ghost the servant at Beechwood saw," said Carver dryly.

He laid some papers and packages on the table, and began carefully to unfold them. "As I say," he continued, "I was sent down here to make inquiries about the criminal plans of this man, Moonshine. That is why I interested myself in bee-keeping and went to stay with Mr. Smith."

There was a silence, and then Devine started and spoke: "You don't seriously mean to say that nice old man – – "

"Come, Mr. Devine," said Carver, with a smile, "you believed a beehive was only a hiding-place for me. Why shouldn't it be a hiding-place for him?"

Devine nodded gloomily, and the detective turned back to his papers. "Suspecting Smith, I wanted to get him out of the way and go through his belongings; so I took advantage of Mr. Bankes's kindness in giving him a joy ride. Searching his house, I found some curious things to be owned by an innocent old rustic interested only in bees. This is one of them."

From the unfolded paper he lifted a long, hairy object almost scarlet in colour – the sort of sham beard that is worn in theatricals.

Beside it lay an old pair of heavy horn-rimmed spectacles.

"But I also found something," continued Carver, "that more directly concerns this house, and must be my excuse for intruding to-night. I found a memorandum, with notes of the names and conjectural value of various pieces of jewellery in the neighbourhood. Immediately after the note of Lady Pulman's tiara was the mention of an emerald necklace belonging to Mrs. Bankes."

Mrs. Bankes, who had hitherto regarded the invasion of her house with an air of supercilious bewilderment, suddenly grew attentive. Her face suddenly looked ten years older and much more intelligent. But before she could speak the impetuous John had risen to his full height like a trumpeting elephant.

"And the tiara's gone already," he roared; "and the necklace — I'm going to see about that necklace!"

"Not a bad idea," said Carver, as the young man rushed from the room; "though, of course, we've been keeping our eyes open since we've been here. Well, it took me a little time to make out the memorandum, which was in cipher, and Father Brown's telephone message from the House came as I was near the end. I asked him to run round here first with the news, and I would follow; and so — — "

His speech was sundered by a scream. Opal was standing up and pointing rigidly at the round window.

"There it is again!" she cried.

For a moment they all saw something — something that cleared the lady of the charges of lying and hysteria not uncommonly brought against her. Thrust out of the slate-blue darkness without, the face was pale, or, perhaps, blanched by pressure against the glass; and the great, glaring eyes, encircled as with rings, gave it rather the look of a great fish out of the dark-blue sea nosing at the port-hole of a ship. But the gills or fins of the fish were a coppery red; they were, in truth, fierce red whiskers and the upper part of a red beard. The next moment it had vanished.

Devine had taken a single stride towards the window when a shout resounded through the house, a shout that seemed to shake it. It seemed almost too deafening to be distinguishable as words; yet it was enough to stop Devine in his stride, and he knew what had happened.

"Necklace gone!" shouted John Bankes, appearing huge and heaving in the doorway, and almost instantly vanishing again with the plunge of a pursuing hound.

"Thief was at the window just now!" cried the detective, who had already darted to the door, following the headlong John, who was already in the garden.

"Be careful," wailed the lady, "they have pistols and things."

"So have I," boomed the distant voice of the dauntless John out of the dark garden.

Devine had, indeed, noticed as the young man plunged past him that he was defiantly brandishing a revolver, and hoped there would be no need for him to so defend himself. But even as he had the thought, came the shock of two shots, as if one answered the other, and awakened a wild flock of echoes in that still suburban garden. They flapped into silence.

"Is John dead?" asked Opal in a low, shuddering voice.

Father Brown had already advanced deeper into the darkness, and stood with his back to them, looking down at something. It was he who answered her.

"No," he said; "it is the other."

Carver had joined him, and for a moment the two figures, the tall and the short, blocked out what view the fitful and stormy moonlight would allow. Then they moved to one side and, the others saw the small, wiry figure lying slightly twisted, as if with its last struggle. The false red beard was thrust upwards, as if scornfully at the sky, and the moon shone on the great sham spectacles of the man who had been called Moonshine.

"What an end," muttered the detective, Carver. "After all his adventures, to be shot almost by accident by a stockbroker in a suburban garden."

The stockbroker himself naturally regarded his own triumph with more solemnity, though not without nervousness.

"I had to do it," he gasped, still panting with exertion. "I'm sorry, he fired at me."

"There will have to be an inquest, of course," said Carver, gravely. "But I think there will be nothing for you to worry about. There's a revolver fallen from his hand with one shot discharged; and he certainly didn't fire after he'd got yours."

By this time they had assembled again in the room, and the detective was getting his papers together for departure. Father Brown was standing opposite to him, looking down at the table, as if in a brown study. Then he spoke abruptly:

"Mr. Carver, you have certainly worked out a very complete case in a very masterly way. I rather suspected your professional business; but I never guessed you would link everything up together so quickly — the bees and the beard and the spectacles and the cipher and the necklace and everything."

"Always satisfactory to get a case really rounded off." said Carver.

"Yes," said Father Brown, still looking at the table. "I admire it very much." Then he added with a modesty verging on nervousness: "It's only fair to you to say that I don't believe a word of it."

Devine leaned forward with sudden interest. "Do you mean you don't believe he is Moonshine, the burglar?"

"I know he is the burglar, but he didn't burgle," answered Father Brown. "I know he didn't come here, or to the great house, to steal jewels, or get shot getting away with them. Where are the jewels?"

"Where they generally are in such cases," said Carver. "He's either hidden them or passed them on to a confederate. This was not a one man job. Of course, my people are searching the garden and warning the district."

"Perhaps," suggested Mrs. Bankes, "the confederate stole the necklace while Moonshine was looking in at the window."

"Why was Moonshine looking in at the window?" asked Father Brown quietly. "Why should he want to look in at the window?"

"Well, what do you think?" cried the cheery John.

"I think," said Father Brown, "that he never did want to look in at the window."

"Then why did he do it?" demanded Carver. "What's the good of talking in the air like that? We've seen the whole thing acted before our very eyes."

"I've seen a good many things acted before my eyes that I didn't believe in," replied the priest. "So have you, on the stage and off."

"Father Brown," said Devine, with a certain respect in his tones, "will you tell us why you can't believe your eyes?"

"Yes, I will try to tell you," answered the priest. Then he said gently:

"You know what I am and what we are. We don't bother you much. We try to be friends with all our neighbours. But you can't think we do nothing. You can't think we know nothing. We mind our own business; but we know our own people. I knew this dead man very well indeed; I was his confessor, and his friend. So far as a man can, I knew his mind when he left that garden to-day; and his mind was like a glass hive full of golden bees. It's an under-statement to say his reformation was sincere. He was one of those great penitents who manage to make more out of penitence than others can make out of virtue. I say I was his confessor; but, indeed, it was I who went to him for comfort. It did me good to be near so

40

good a man. And when I saw him lying there dead in the garden, it seemed to me as if certain strange words that were said of old were spoken over him aloud in my ear. They might well be; for if ever a man went straight to heaven, it might be he."

"Hang it all," said John Bankes restlessly, "after all, he was a convicted thief."

"Yes," said Father Brown; "and only a convicted thief has ever in this world heard that assurance: 'This night shalt thou be with Me in Paradise.'"

Nobody seemed to know what to do with the silence that followed, until Devine said, abruptly, at last:

"Then how in the world would you explain it all?"

The priest shook his head. "I can't explain it at all, just yet," he said, simply. "I can see one or two odd things, but I don't understand them. As yet I've nothing to go on to prove the man's innocence, except the man. But I'm quite sure I'm right."

He sighed, and put out his hand for his big, black hat. As he removed it he remained gazing at the table with rather a new expression, his round, straight-haired head cocked at a new angle. It was rather as if some curious animal had come out of his hat, as out of the hat of a conjurer. But the others, looking at the table, could see nothing there but the detective's documents and the tawdry old property beard and spectacles.

"Lord bless us," muttered Father Brown, "and he's lying outside dead, in a beard and spectacles." He swung round suddenly upon Devine. "Here's something to follow up, if you want to know. Why did he have two beards?"

With that he bustled in his undignified way out of the room; but Devine was now devoured with curiosity, and pursued him into the front garden.

"I can't tell you now," said Father Brown. "I'm not sure, and I'm bothered about what to do. Come round and see me to-morrow, and I may be able to tell you the whole tiling. It may already be settled for me, and — did you hear that noise?"

"A motor-car starting," remarked Devine.

"Mr. John Bankes's motor-car," said the priest. "I believe it goes very fast."

"He certainly is of that opinion." said Devine, with a smile.

"It will go far, as well as fast, to-night," said Father Brown.

41

"And what do you mean by that?" demanded the other.

"I mean it will not return," replied the priest. "John Bankes suspected something of what I knew from what I said. John Bankes has gone and the emeralds and all the other jewels with him."

Next day, Devine found. Father Brown moving to and fro in front of the row of beehives, sadly, but with a certain serenity.

"I've been telling the bees," he said. "You know one has to tell the bees!" Those singing masons building roofs of gold.' What a line!" Then more abruptly. "He would like the bees looked after."

"I hope he doesn't want the human beings neglected, when the whole swarm is buzzing with curiosity," observed the young man. "You were quite right when you said that Bankes was gone with the jewels; but I don't know how you knew, or even what there was to be known."

Father Brown blinked benevolently at the bee-hives and said:

"One sort of stumbles on things, and there was one stumbling-block at the start. I was puzzled by poor Barnard being shot up at Beechwood House. Now, even when Michael was a master criminal, he made it a point of honour, even a point of vanity, to succeed without any killing. It seemed extraordinary that when he had become a sort of saint he should go out of his way to commit the sin he had despised when he was a sinner. The rest of the business puzzled me to the last; I could make nothing out of it, except that it wasn't true. Then I had a belated gleam of sense when I saw the beard and goggles and remembered the thief had come in another beard with other goggles. Now, of course, it was just possible that he had duplicates; but it was at least a coincidence that he used neither the old glasses nor the old beard, both in good repair. Again, it was just possible that he went out without them and had to procure new ones; but it was unlikely. There was nothing to make him go motoring with Bankes at all; if he was really going burgling, he could have taken his outfit easily in his pocket. Besides, beards don't grow on bushes. He would have found it hard to get such things anywhere in the time.

"No, the more I thought of it the more I felt there was something funny about his having a completely new outfit. And then the truth began to dawn on me by reason, which I knew already by instinct. He never did go out with Bankes with any intention of putting on the disguise. He never did put on the disguise. Somebody else manufactured the disguise at leisure, and then put it on him."

"Put it on him!" repeated Devine. "How the devil could they?"

"Let us go back," said Father Brown, "and look at the thing through another window — the window through which the young lady saw the ghost."

"The ghost!" repeated the other, with a slight start.

"She called it the ghost," said the little man, with composure, "and perhaps she was not so far wrong. It's quite true that she is what they call psychic. Her only mistake is in thinking that being psychic is being spiritual. Some animals are psychic; anyhow, she is a sensitive, and she was right when she felt that the face at the window had a son of horrible halo of deathly things."

"You mean — —" began Devine.

"I mean it was a dead man who looked in at the window," said Father Brown. "It was a dead man who crawled round more than one house, looking in at more than one window. Creepy, wasn't it? But in one way it was the reverse of a ghost; for it was not the antic of the soul freed from the body. It was the antic of the body freed from the soul."

He blinked again at the beehive and continued: "But, I suppose, the shortest explanation is to take it from the standpoint of the man who did it. You know the man who did it. John Bankes."

"The very last man I should have thought of," said Devine.

"The very first man I thought of," said Father Brown; "in so far as I had any right to think of anybody. My friend, there are no good or bad social types or trades. Any man can be a murderer like poor John; any man, even the same man, can be a saint like poor Michael. But if there is one type that tends at times to be more utterly godless than another, it is that rather brutal sort of business man. He has no social ideal, let alone religion; he has neither the gentleman's traditions nor the trade unionist's class loyalty. All his boasts about getting good bargains were practically boasts of having cheated people. His snubbing of his sister's poor little attempts at mysticism was detestable. Her mysticism was all nonsense; but he only hated spiritualism because it was spirituality. Anyhow, there's no doubt he was the villain of the piece; the only interest is in a rather original piece of villainy. It was really a new and unique motive for murder. It was the motive of using the corpse as a stage property — a sort of hideous doll or dummy. At the start he conceived a plan of killing Michael in the motor, merely to take him home and pretend to have killed him in the garden. But ail sorts of fantastic finishing touches followed quite naturally from the primary fact; that he had at his disposal in a closed car at night the dead body of a recognized and recognizable burglar. He could leave his finger-prints and foot-prints; he could lean the familiar face against windows and take it away. You will notice that Moonshine ostensibly appeared and vanished while Bankes was ostensibly out of the room looking for the emerald necklace.

"Finally, he had only to tumble the corpse on to the lawn, fire a shot from each pistol, and there he was. It might never have been found out but for a guess about the two beards."

"Why had your friend Michael kept the old beard?" Devine said thoughtfully. "That seems to me questionable."

"To me, who knew him, it seems quite inevitable," replied Father Brown. "His whole attitude was like that wig that he wore. There was no disguise about his disguises. He didn't want the old disguise any more, but he wasn't frightened of it; he would have felt it false to destroy the false beard. It would have been like hiding; and he was not hiding. He was not hiding from God; he was not hiding from himself. He was in the broad daylight. If they'd taken him back to prison, he'd still have been quite happy. He was not whitewashed, but washed white. There was something very strange about him; almost as strange as the grotesque dance of death through which he was dragged after he was dead. When he moved to and fro smiling among these beehives, even then, in a most radiant and shining sense, he was dead. He was out of the judgment of this world."

There was a short pause, and then Devine shrugged his shoulders and said: "It all comes back to bees and wasps looking very much alike in this world, doesn't it?"

IV: THE SONG OF THE FLYING FISH

THE soul of Mr. Peregrine Smart hovered like a fly round one possession and one joke. It might be considered a mild joke, for it consisted merely of asking people if they had seen his goldfish. It might also be considered an expensive joke; but it is doubtful whether he was not secretly more attached to the joke than to the evidence of expenditure. In talking to his neighbours in the little group of new houses that had grown up round the old village green, he lost no time in turning the conversation in the direction of his hobby. To Dr. Burdock, a rising biologist with a resolute chin and hair brushed back like a German's, Mr. Smart made the easy transition. "You are interested in natural history; have you seen my goldfish?" To so orthodox an evolutionist as Dr. Burdock doubtless all nature was one; but at first sight the link was not close, as he was a specialist who had concentrated entirely upon the primitive ancestry of the giraffe. To Father Brown, from a church in the neighbouring provincial town, he traced a rapid train of thought which touched on the topics of "Rome—St. Peter—fisherman—fish—goldfish." In talking to Mr. Imlack Smith, the bank manager, a slim and sallow gentleman of dressy appearance but quiet demeanour, he violently wrenched the conversation to the subject of the gold standard, from which it was merely a step to goldfish. In talking to that brilliant Oriental traveller and scholar. Count Yvon de Lara (whose title was French and his face rather Russian, not to say Tartar), the versatile conversationalist showed an intense and intelligent interest in the Ganges and the Indian Ocean, leading naturally to the possible presence of goldfish in those waters.

From Mr. Harry Hartopp, the very rich but very shy and silent young gentleman who had recently come down from London, he had at last extorted the information that the embarrassed youth in question was not interested in fishing, and had then added: "Talking about fishing, have you seen my goldfish?"

The peculiar thing about the goldfish was that they were made of gold. They were part of an eccentric but expensive toy, said to have been made by the freak of some rich Eastern prince, and Mr. Smart had picked it up at some sale or in some curiosity shop, such as he frequented for the purpose of lumbering up his house with unique and useless things. From the other end of the room it looked like a rather unusually large bowl containing rather unusually large living fish; a closer inspection showed it to be a huge bubble of beautifully blown Venetian glass, very thin and delicately clouded with faintly iridescent colour, in the tinted twilight of which hung grotesque golden fishes with great rubies for eyes. The whole thing was undoubtedly worth a great deal in solid material; how much more would depend upon the waves of lunacy passing over the world of collectors. Mr. Smart's new secretary, a young man named Francis Boyle, though an Irishman and not credited with caution, was mildly surprised at his talking so freely of the gems of his collection to the group of comparative strangers who happened to have alighted in a rather nomadic fashion in the neighbourhood; for collectors are commonly vigilant and sometimes secretive. In the course of settling down to his new duties, Mr. Boyle found he was not alone in this sentiment, and that in others, it passed from a mild wonder to a grave disapproval.

"It's a wonder his throat isn't cut," said Mr. Smart's valet, Harris, not without a hypothetical relish, almost as if he had said, in a purely artistic sense: "It's a pity."

"It's extraordinary how he leaves things about," said Mr. Smart's head clerk, Jameson, who had come up from the office to assist the new secretary, "and he won't even put up those ramshackle old bars across his ramshackle old door."

"It's all very well with Father Brown and the doctor," said Mr. Smart's housekeeper, with a certain vigorous vagueness that marked her opinions, "but when it comes to foreigners, I call it tempting providence. It isn't only the Count, either; that man at the bank looks to me much too yellow to be English."

"Well, that young Hartopp is English enough," said Boyle good-humouredly, "to the extent of not having a word to say for himself."

"He thinks the more," said the housekeeper. "He may not be exactly a foreigner, but he is not such a fool as he looks. Foreign is as foreign does, I say," she added darkly.

Her disapproval would probably have deepened if she had heard the conversation, in her master's drawing-room that afternoon, a conversation of which the goldfish were the text, though the offensive foreigner tended more and more to be the central figure. It was not that he spoke so very

46

much; but even his silences had something positive about them. He looked the more massive for sitting in a sort of heap on a heap of cushions, and in the deepening twilight his wide Mongolian face seemed faintly luminous, like a moon. Perhaps his background brought out something atmospherically Asiatic about his face and figure, for the room was a chaos of more or less costly curiosities, amid which could be seen the crooked curves and burning colours of countless Eastern weapons, Eastern pipes and vessels, Eastern musical instruments and illuminated manuscripts. Anyhow, as the conversation proceeded, Boyle felt more and more that the figure seated on the cushions and dark against the twilight had the exact outline of a huge image of Buddha.

The conversation was general enough, for all the little local group were present. They were, indeed, often in the habit of dropping in at each other's houses, and by this time constituted a sort of club, of people coming from the four or five houses standing round the green. Of these houses Peregrine Smart's was the oldest, largest, and most picturesque; it straggled down almost the whole of one side of the square, leaving only room for a small villa, inhabited by a retired colonel named Varney, who was reported to be an invalid, and certainly was never seen to go abroad. At right angles to these stood two or three shops that served the simpler needs of the hamlet, and at the corner the inn of the Blue Dragon, at which Mr. Hartopp, the stranger from London, was staying. On the opposite side were three houses, one rented by the Count de Lara, one by Dr. Burdock, and the third still standing empty. On the fourth side was the bank, with an adjoining house for the bank manager, and a line offence enclosing some land that was let for building. It was thus a very self-contained group, and the comparative emptiness of the open ground for miles round it threw the members more and more on each other's society. That afternoon, one stranger had indeed broken into the magic circle: a hatchet-faced fellow with fierce tufts of eyebrows and moustache, and so shabbily dressed that he must have been a millionaire or a duke if he had really (as was alleged) come down to do business with the old collector. But he was known, at the Blue Dragon at least, as Mr. Harmer.

To him had been recounted anew the glories of the gilded fish and the criticisms regarding their custody.

"People are always telling me I ought to lock them up more carefully," observed Mr. Smart, cocking an eyebrow over his shoulder at the dependant who stood there holding some papers from the office. Smart was a round-faced, round-bodied little old man rather like a bald parrot. "Jameson and Harris and the rest are always at me to bar the doors as if it were a mediaeval fortress, though really these rotten old rusty bars are too mediaeval to keep anybody out, I should think. I prefer to trust to luck and the local police."

"It is not always the best bars that keep people out," said the Count. "It all depends on who's trying to get in. There was an ancient Hindu hermit who lived naked in a cave and passed through the three armies that encircled the Mogul and took the great ruby out of the tyrant's turban, and went back unscathed like a shadow. For he wished to teach the great how small are the laws of space and time."

"When we really study the small laws of space and time," said Dr. Burdock dryly, "we generally find out how those tricks are done. Western science has let in daylight on a good deal of Eastern magic. Doubtless a great deal can be done with hypnotism and suggestion, to say nothing of sleight-of-hand."

"The ruby was not in the royal tent," observed the Count in his dream fashion; "but he found it among a hundred tents."

"Can't all that be explained by telepathy?" asked the doctor sharply. The question sounded the sharper because it was followed by a heavy silence, almost as if the distinguished Oriental traveller had, with imperfect politeness, gone to sleep.

"I beg your pardon," he said rousing himself with a sudden smile. "I had forgotten we were talking with words. In the east we talk with thoughts, and so we never misunderstand each other. It is strange how you people worship words and are satisfied with words. What difference does it make to a thing that you now call it telepathy, as you once called it tomfoolery? If a man climbs into the sky on a mango-tree, how is it altered by saying it is only levitation, instead of saying it is only lies. If a medieval witch waved a wand and turned me into a blue baboon, you would say it was only atavism."

The doctor looked for a moment as if he might say that it would not be so great a change after all. But before his irritation could find that or any other vent, the man called Harmer interrupted gruffly:

"It's true enough those Indian conjurers can do queer things, but I notice they generally do them in India. Confederates, perhaps, or merely mass psychology. I don't think those tricks have ever been played in an English village, and I should say our friend's goldfish were quite safe."

"I will tell you a story," said de Lara, in his motionless way, "which happened not in India, but outside an English barrack in the most modernized part of Cairo. A sentinel was standing inside the grating of an iron gateway looking out between the bars on to the street. There appeared outside the gate a beggar, barefoot and in native rags, who asked him, in English that was startlingly distinct and refined, for a certain official document kept in the building for safety. The soldier told the man, of that he could not come inside; and the man answered, smiling: course, 'What is inside and what is outside?' The soldier was still staring scornfully through the iron grating when he gradually realized that, though neither he nor the gate had moved, he was actually standing in the street and looking in at the barrack yard, where the beggar stood still and smiling and equally motionless. Then, when the beggar turned towards the building, the sentry awoke to such sense as he had left, and shouted a warning to all the soldiers within the gated enclosure to hold the prisoner fast. 'You won't get out of there anyhow,' he said vindictively. Then the beggar said in his silvery voice: 'What is outside and what is inside?' And the soldier, still glaring through the same bars, saw that they were once more between him and the street, where the beggar stood free and smiling with a paper in his hand."

Mr. Imlack Smith, the bank manager, was looking at the carpet with his dark sleek head bowed, and he spoke for the first time.

"Did anything happen about the paper?" he asked.

"Your professional instincts are correct, sir," said the Count with grim affability. "It was a paper of considerable financial importance. Its consequences were international."

"I hope they don't occur often," said young Hartopp gloomily.

"I do not touch the political side," said the Count serenely, "but only the philosophical. It illustrates how the wise man can get behind time and space and turn the levers of them, so to speak, so that the whole world turns round before our eyes. But is it so hard for you people to believe that spiritual powers are really more powerful than material ones."

"Well," said old Smart cheerfully, "I don't profess to be an authority on spiritual powers. What do you say, Father Brown?"

"The only thing that strikes me," answered the little priest, "is that all the supernatural acts we have yet heard of seem to be thefts. And stealing by spiritual methods seem to me much the same as stealing by material ones."

"Father Brown is a Philistine," said the smiling Smith.

"I have a sympathy with the tribe," said Father Brown. "A Philistine is only a man who is right without knowing why."

"All this is too clever for me," said Hartopp heartily.

"Perhaps," said Father Brown with a smile, "you would like to speak without words, as the Count suggests. He would begin by saying nothing in a pointed fashion, and you would retort with a burst of taciturnity."

"Something might be done with music," murmured the Count dreamily. "It would be better than all these words."

"Yes, I might understand that better," said the young man in a low voice.

Boyle had followed the conversation with curious attention, for there was something in the demeanour of more than one of the talkers that seemed to him significant or even odd. As the talk drifted to music, with an appeal to the dapper bank manager (who was an amateur musician of some merit), the young secretary awoke with a start to his secretarial duties, and reminded his employer that the head clerk was still standing patiently with the papers in his hand.

"Oh, never mind about those just now, Jameson," said Smart rather hurriedly. "Only something about my account; I'll see Mr. Smith about it later. You were saying that the 'cello, Mr. Smith — — "

But the cold breath of business had sufficed to disperse the fumes of transcendental talk, and the guests began one after another to say farewell. Only Mr. Imlack Smith, bank manager and musician, remained to the last; and when the rest were gone he and his host went into the inner room, where the goldfish were kept, and closed the door.

The house was long and narrow, with a covered balcony running along the first floor, which consisted mostly of a sort of suite of rooms used by the householder himself, his bedroom and dressing-room, and an inner room in which his very valuable treasures were sometimes stored for the night instead of being left in the rooms below. This balcony, like the insufficiently barred door below it, was a matter of concern to the housekeeper and the head clerk and the others who lamented the carelessness of the collector; but, in truth, that cunning old gentleman was more careful than he seemed. He professed no great belief in the antiquated fastenings of the old house, which the housekeeper lamented to see rusting in idleness, but he had an eye to the more important point of strategy. He always put his favourite goldfish in the room at the back of his bedroom for the night, and slept in front of it, as it were, with a pistol under his pillow. And when Boyle and Jameson, awaiting his return from the tete-a-tete, at length saw the door open and their employer reappear, he was carrying the great glass bowl as reverently as it if had been the relic of a saint.

Outside, the last edges of the sunset still clung to the corners of the green square; but inside, a lamp had already been kindled; and in the mingling of the two lights the coloured globe glowed like some monstrous jewel, and the fantastic outlines of the fiery fishes seemed to give it, indeed, something of the mystery of a talisman, like strange shapes seen by a seer in the crystal of doom. Over the old man's shoulder the olive face of Imlack Smith stared like a sphinx.

"I am going up to London to-night, Mr. Boyle," said old Smart, with more gravity than he commonly showed. "Mr. Smith and I are catching the six-forty-five. I should prefer you, Jameson, to sleep upstairs in my room to-night; if you put the bowl in the back room as usual, it will be quite safe then. Not that I suppose anything could possibly happen."

"Anything may happen anywhere," said the smiling Mr. Smith. "I think you generally take a gun to bed with you. Perhaps you had better leave it behind in this case."

Peregrine Smart did not reply, and they passed out of the house on to the road round the village green.

The secretary and the head clerk slept that night as directed in their employer's bedroom. To speak more strictly, Jameson, the head clerk, slept in a bed in the dressing-room, but the door stood open between, and the two rooms running along the front were practically one. Only the bedroom had a long French window giving on the balcony, and an entrance at the back into the inner apartment where the goldfish bowl had been placed for safety. Boyle dragged his bed right across so as to bar this entrance, put the revolver under his pillow, and then undressed and went to bed, feeling that he had taken all possible precautions against an impossible or improbable event. He did not see why there should be any particular danger of normal burglary; and as for the spiritual burglary that figured in the traveller's tales of the Count de Lara, if his thoughts ran on them so near to sleep it was because they were such stuff as dreams are made of. They soon turned into dreams with intervals of dreamless slumber. The old clerk was a little more restless as usual; but after fussing about a little longer and repeating some of his favourite regrets and warnings, he also retired to his bed in the same manner and slept. The moon brightened and grew dim again above the green square and the grey blocks of houses in a solitude and silence that seemed to have no human witness; and it was when the white cracks of daybreak had already appeared in the corners of the grey sky that the thing happened.

Boyle, being young, was naturally both the healthier and the heavier sleeper of the two. Though active enough when he was once awake, he always had a load to lift in waking. Moreover, he had dreams of the sort that cling to the emerging minds like the dim tentacles of an octopus. They were a medley of many things, including his last look from the balcony across the four grey roads and the green square. But the pattern of them changed and shifted and turned dizzily, to the accompaniment of a low grinding noise, which sounded somehow like a subterranean river, and may have been no more than old Mr. Jameson snoring in the dressing-room. But in the dreamer's mind all that murmur and motion was vaguely connected with the words of the Count de Lara, about a wisdom that could hold the levers of time and space and turn the world. In the dream it seemed as if a vast murmuring machinery under the world were really moving whole landscapes hither and thither, so that the ends of the earth might appear in a man's front-garden, or his own front-garden be exiled beyond the sea.

The first complete impressions he had were the words of a song, with a rather thin metallic accompaniment; they were sung in a foreign accent and a voice that was still strange and yet faintly familiar. And yet he could hardly feel sure that he was not making up poetry in his sleep.

Over the land and over the sea
My flying fishes will come to me,
For the note is not of the world that wakes them,
But in — —

He struggled to his feet and saw that his fellow-guardian was already out of bed; Jameson was peering out of the long window on to the balcony and calling out sharply to someone in the street below.

"Who's that?" he called out sharply. "What do you want?"

He turned to Boyle in agitation, saying: "There's somebody prowling about just outside. I knew it wasn't safe. I'm going down to bar that front door, whatever they say."

He ran downstairs in a flutter and Boyle could hear the clattering of the bars upon the front door; but Boyle himself stepped out upon the balcony and looked out on the long grey road that led up to the house, and he thought he was still dreaming.

Upon that grey road leading across that empty moor and through that little English hamlet, there had appeared a figure that might have stepped straight out of the jungle or the bazaar — a figure out of one of the Count's fantastic stories; a figure out of the "Arabian Nights." The rather ghostly grey twilight which begins to define and yet to discolour everything when the light in the east has ceased to be localized, lifted slowly like a veil of grey gauze and showed him a figure wrapped in outlandish raiment. A scarf of a strange sea-blue, vast and voluminous, went round the head like a turban, and then again round the chin, giving rather the general character of a hood; so far as the face was concerned it had a the effects of a mask. For the raiment round the head was drawn close as a veil; and the head itself was bowed over a queer-looking musical instrument made of silver or steel, and shaped like a deformed or crooked violin. It was played with something like a silver comb, and the notes were curiously thin and keen.

Before Boyle could open his mouth, the same haunting alien accent came from under the shadow of the burnous, singing-words of the same sort:

As the golden birds go back to the tree
My golden fishes return to me.
Return — —

"You've no right here," called out Boyle in exasperation, hardly knowing what he said.

"I have a right to the goldfish," said the stranger, speaking more like King Solomon than an unsandalled Bedouin in a ragged blue cloak. "And they will come to me. Come!"

He struck his strange fiddle as his voice rose sharply on the word. There was a pang of sound that seemed to pierce the mind, and then there came a fainter sound, like an answer: a vibrant whisper. It came from the dark room behind where the bowl of goldfish was standing.

Boyle turned towards it; and even as he turned the echo in the inner room changed to a long tingling sound like an electric bell, and then to a faint crash. It was still a matter of seconds since he had challenged the man from the balcony; but the old clerk had already regained the top of the stairs, panting a little, for he was an elderly gentleman.

"I've locked up the door, anyhow," he said.

"The stable door," said Boyle out of the darkness of the inner room.

Jameson followed him into that apartment and found him staring down at the floor, which was covered with a litter of coloured glass like the curved bits of a broken rainbow.

"What do you mean by the stable door?" began Jameson.

"I mean that the steed is stolen," answered Boyle. "The flying steeds. The flying fishes our Arab friend outside has just whistled to like so many performing puppies."

"But how could he?" exploded the old clerk, as if such events were hardly respectable.

"Well, they're gone," said Boyle shortly. "The broken bowl is here, which would have taken a long time to open properly, but only a second to smash. But the fish are gone, God knows how, though I think our friend ought to be asked."

"We are wasting time," said the distracted Jameson. "We ought to be after him at once."

"Much better be telephoning the police at once," answered Boyle. "They ought to outstrip him in a flash with motors and telephones that go a good deal farther than we should ever get, running through the village in our nightgowns. But it may be there are things even the police cars and wires won't outstrip."

While Jameson was talking to the police-station through the telephone in an agitated voice, Boyle went out again on to the balcony and hastily scanned that grey landscape of daybreak. There was no trace of the man in the turban, and no other sign of life, except some faint stirrings an expert might have recognized in the hotel of the Blue Dragon. Only Boyle, for the first time, noted consciously something that he had all along been noting unconsciously. It was like a fact struggling in the submerged mind and demanding its own meaning. It was simply the fact that the grey landscape had never been entirely grey; there was one gold spot amid its stripes of colourless colour, a lamp lighted in one of the houses on the other side of the green-Something, perhaps irrational, told him that it had been burning through all the hours of the darkness and was only fading with the dawn. He counted the houses, and his calculation brought out a result which seemed to fit in with something, he knew not what. Anyhow, it was apparently the house of the Count Yvon de Lara.

Inspector Pinner had arrived with several policemen, and done several things of a rapid and resolute sort, being conscious that the very absurdity of the costly trinkets might give the case considerable prominence in the newspapers. He had examined everything, measured, everything, taken down everybody's deposition, taken everybody's finger -prints, put everybody's back up, and found himself at the end left facing a fact which he could not believe. An Arab from the desert had walked up the public road and stopped in front of the house of Mr. Peregrine Smart, where a bowl of artificial goldfish was kept in an inner room; he had then sung or recited a little poem, and the bowl had exploded like a bomb and the fishes vanished into thin air. Nor did it soothe the inspector to be told by a foreign Count — in a soft, purring voice — that the bounds of experience were being enlarged.

Indeed, the attitude of each member of the little group was characteristic enough. Peregrine Smart himself had come back from London the next morning to hear the news of his loss. Naturally he admitted a shock; but it was typical of something sporting and spirited in the little old gentleman, something that always made his small strutting figure look like a cock-sparrow's, that he showed more vivacity in the search than depression at the loss. The man named Harmer, who had come to the village on purpose to buy the goldfish, might be excused for being a little testy on learning they were not there to be bought. But, in truth, his rather aggressive moustache and eyebrows seemed to bristle with something more definite than disappointment, and the eyes that darted over the company were bright with a vigilance that might well be suspicion. The sallow face of the bank manager, who had also returned from London though by a later train, seemed again and again to attract those shining and shifting eyes like a magnet. Of the two remaining figures of the original circle. Father Brown was generally silent when he was not spoken to, and the dazed Hartopp was often silent even when he was.

But the Count was not a man to let anything pass that gave an apparent advantage to his views. He smiled at his rationalistic rival, the doctor, in the manner of one who knows how it is possible to be irritating by being ingratiating.

"You will admit, doctor," he said, "that at least some of the stories you thought so improbable look a little more realistic to-day than they did yesterday. When a man as ragged as those I described is able, by speaking a word, to dissolve a solid vessel inside the four walls of the house he stands outside, it might perhaps be called an example of what I said about spiritual powers and material barriers."

"And it might be called an example of what I said," said the doctor sharply, "about a little scientific knowledge being enough to show how the tricks are done."

"Do you really mean, doctor," asked Smart in some excitement, "that you can throw any scientific light on this mystery?"

"I can throw light on what the Count calls a mystery," said the doctor, "because it is not a mystery at all. That part of it is plain enough. A sound is only a wave of vibration, and certain vibrations can break glass, if the sound is of a certain kind and the glass of a certain kind. The man did not stand in the road and think, which the Count tells us is the ideal method when Orientals want a little chat. He sang out what he wanted, quite loud, and struck a shrill note on an instrument. It is similar to many experiments by which glass of special composition has been cracked."

"Such as the experiment," said the Count lightly, "by which several lumps of solid gold have suddenly ceased to exist."

"Here comes Inspector Pinner," said Boyle. "Between ourselves, I think he would regard the doctor's natural explanation as quite as much of a fairy tale as the Count's preternatural one. A very sceptical intellect, Mr. Pinner's, especially about me. I rather think I am under suspicion."

"I think we are all under suspicion," said the Count.

It was the presence of this suspicion in his own case that led Boyle to seek the personal advice of Father Brown. They were walking round the village green together, some hours later in the day, when the priest, who was frowning thoughtfully at the ground as he listened, suddenly stopped.

"Do you see that?" he asked. "Somebody's been washing the pavement here—just this little strip of pavement outside Colonel Varney's house. I wonder whether that was done yesterday."

Father Brown looked rather earnestly at the house, which was high and narrow, and carried rows of striped sun-blinds of gay but already faded colours. The chinks or crannies that gave glimpses of the interior looked all the darker; indeed, they looked almost black in contrast with the facade thus golden in the morning light.

"That is Colonel Varney's house, isn't it?" he asked. "He comes from the East, too, I fancy. What sort of man is he?"

"I've never even seen him," answered Boyle. "I don't think anybody's seen him, except Dr. Burdock, and I rather fancy the doctor doesn't see him more than he need."

"Well, I'm going to see him for a minute," said Father Brown.

The big front door opened and swallowed the small priest, and his friend stood staring at it in a dazed and irrational manner, as if wondering whether it would ever open again. It opened in a few minutes, and Father Brown emerged, still smiling, and continued his slow and pottering progress round the square of roads. Sometimes he seemed to have forgotten the matter in hand altogether, for he would make passing remarks on historical and social questions, or on the prospects of development in the district. He remarked on the soil used for the beginning of a new road by the bank; he looked across the old village green with a vague expression.

"Common land. I suppose people ought to feed their pigs and geese on it, if they had any pigs or geese; as it is, it seems to feed nothing but nettles and thistles. What a pity that what was supposed to be a sort of large meadow has been turned into a small and petty wilderness. That's Dr. Burdock's house opposite, isn't it?"

"Yes," answered Boyle, almost jumping at this abrupt postscript.

"Very well," answered Father Brown, "then I think we'll go indoors again."

As they opened the front door of Smart's house and mounted the stairs, Boyle repeated to his companion many details of the drama enacted there at daybreak.

"I suppose you didn't doze off again?" asked Father Brown, "giving time for somebody to scale the balcony while Jameson ran down to secure the door."

"No," answered Boyle; "I am sure of that. I woke up to hear Jameson challenging the stranger from the balcony; then I heard him running downstairs and putting up the bars, and then in two strides I was on the balcony myself."

"Or could he have slipped in between you from another angle? Are there any other entrances besides the front entrance?"

"Apparently there are not," said Boyle gravely.

"I had better make sure, don't you think?" asked Father Brown apologetically, and scuttled softly downstairs again. Boyle remained in the front bedroom gazing rather doubtfully after him. After a comparatively brief interval the round and rather rustic visage appeared again at the head of the stairs, looking rather like a turnip ghost with a broad grin.

"No; I think that settles the matter of entrances," said the turnip ghost, cheerfully. "And now, I think, having got everything in a tight box, so to speak, we can take stock of what we've got. It's rather a curious business."

"Do you think," asked Boyle, 'that the Count or the colonel, or any of these Eastern travellers have anything to do with it? Do you think it is— preternatural?"

"I will grant you this," said the priest gravely, "if the Count, or the colonel, or any of your neighbours did dress up in Arab masquerade and creep up to this house in the dark—then it was preternatural."

"What do you mean? Why?"

"Because the Arab left no footprints," answered Father Brown. "The colonel on the one side and the banker on the other are the nearest of your neighbours. That loose red soil is between you and the bank, it would print off bare feet like a plaster cast and probably leave red marks everywhere. I braved the colonel's curry-seasoned temper to verify the fact that the front pavement was washed yesterday and not to -day; it was wet enough to make wet footprints all along the road. Now, if the visitor were the Count or the doctor in the houses opposite, he might possibly, of course, have come across the common. But he must have found it exceedingly uncomfortable with bare feet, for it is, as I remarked, one mass of thorns and thistles and stinging nettles. He would surely have pricked himself and probably left traces of it. Unless, as you say, he was a preternatural being."

Boyle looked steadily at the grave and indecipherable face of his clerical friend.

"Do you mean that he was?" he asked, at length.

"There is one general truth to remember," said Father Brown, after a pause. "A thing can sometimes be too close to be seen, as, for instance, a man cannot see himself. There was a man who had a fly in his eye when he looked through the telescope, and he discovered that there was a most incredible dragon in the moon. And I am told that if a man hears the exact reproduction of his own voice it sounds like the voice of a stranger. In the same way, if anything is right in the foreground of our life we hardly see it, and if we did we might think it quite odd. If the thing in the foreground got into the middle distance, we should probably think it had come from the remote distance. Just come outside the house again for a moment. I want to show you how it looks from another standpoint."

He had already risen, and as they descended the stairs he continued his remarks in a rather groping fashion as if he were thinking aloud.

"The Count and the Asiatic atmosphere all come in, because, in a case like this, everything depends on the preparation of the mind. A man can reach a condition in which a brick, falling on his head, will seem to be a

Babylonian brick carved with cuneiform, and dropped from the Hanging Gardens of Babylon, so that he will never even look at the brick and see it is of one pattern with the bricks or his own house. So in your case – – "

"What does this mean?" interrupted Boyle, staring and pointing at the entrance. "What in the name of wonder does it mean? The door is barred again."

He was staring at the front door by which they had entered but a little while before, and across which stood, once more, the great dark bands of rusty iron which had once, as he had said, locked the stable door too late. There was something darkly and dumbly ironic in those old fastenings closing behind them and imprisoning them as if of their own motion.

"Oh those!" said Father Brown casually. "I put up those bars myself, just now. Didn't you hear me?"

"No," answered Boyle, staring. "I heard nothing."

"Well, I rather thought you wouldn't," said the other equably. "There's really no reason why anybody upstairs should hear those bars being put up. A sort of hook fits easily into a sort of hole. When you're quite close you hear a dull click; but that's all. The only thing that makes any noise a man could hear upstairs, is this."

And he lifted the bar out of its socket and let it fall with a clang at the side of the door,

"It does make a noise if you unbar the door," said Father Brown gravely, "even if you do it pretty carefully."

"You mean – "

"I mean," said Father Brown, "that what you heard upstairs was Jameson opening the door and not shutting it. And now let's open the door ourselves and go outside."

When they stood outside in the street, under the balcony, the little priest resumed his previous explanation as coolly as if it had been a chemical lecture.

"I was saying that a man may be in the mood to look for something very distant, and not realize that it is something very close, something very close to himself, perhaps something very like himself. It was a strange and outlandish thing that you saw when you looked down at this road. I suppose it never occurred to you to consider what he saw when he looked up at that balcony?"

Boyle was staring at the balcony and did not answer, and the other added:

"You thought it very wild and wonderful that an Arab should come through civilized England with bare feet. You did not remember that at the same moment you had bare feet yourself."

Boyle at last found words, and it was to repeat words already spoken. "Jameson opened the door," he said mechanically.

"Yes," assented, his friend. "Jameson opened the door and came out into the road in his nightclothes, just as you came out on the balcony. He caught up two things that you had seen a hundred times: the length of old blue curtain that he wrapped round his head, and the Oriental musical instrument you must have often seen in that heap of Oriental curiosities. The rest was atmosphere and acting, very fine acting, for he is a very fine artist in crime."

"Jameson!" exclaimed Boyle incredulously. "He was such a dull old stick that I never even noticed him."

"Precisely," said the priest, "he was an artist. If he could act a wizard or a troubadour for six minutes, do you think he could not act a clerk for six weeks?"

"I am still not quite sure of his object," said Boyle.

"His object has been achieved," replied Father Brown, "or very nearly achieved. He had taken the goldfish already, of course, as he had twenty chances of doing. But if he had simply taken, them, everybody would have realized that he had twenty chances of doing it. By creating a mysterious magician from the end of the earth, he set everybody's thoughts wandering far afield to Arabia and India, so that you yourself can hardly believe that the whole thing was so near home. It was too close to you to be seen."

"If this is true," said Boyle, "it was an extraordinary risk to run, and he had to cut it very fine. It's true I never heard the man in the street say anything while Jameson was talking from the balcony, so I suppose that was all a fake. And I suppose it's true that there was time for him to get outside before I had fully woken up and got out on to the balcony."

"Every crime depends on somebody not waking up too soon," replied Father Brown; "and in every sense most of us wake up too late. I, for one, have woken up much too late. For I imagine he's bolted long ago, just before or just after they took his finger-prints."

"You woke up before anybody else, anyhow," said Boyle, "and I should never have woken up in that sense. Jameson was so correct and colourless that I forgot all about him."

"Beware of the man you forget," replied his friend; "he is the one man who has you entirely at a disadvantage. But I did not suspect him, either, until you told me how you had heard him barring the door."

"Anyhow, we owe it all to you," said Boyle warmly.

"You owe it all to Mrs. Robinson," said Father Brown with a smile.

"Mrs. Robinson?" questioned the wondering secretary. "You don't mean the housekeeper?"

"Beware of the woman you forget, and even more," answered the other. "This man was a very high-class criminal; he had been an excellent actor, and therefore he was a good psychologist. A man like the Count never hears any voice but his own; but this man could listen, when you had all forgotten he was there, and gather exactly the right materials for his romance and know exactly the right note to strike to lead you all astray. But he made one bad mistake in the psychology of Mrs. Robinson, the housekeeper."

"I don't understand," answered Boyle, "what she can have to do with it."

"Jameson did not expect the doors to be barred," said Father Brown. "He knew that a lot of men, especially careless men like you and your employer, could go on saying for days that something ought to be done, or might as well be done. But if you convey to a woman that something ought to be done, there is always a dreadful danger that she will suddenly do it."

V: THE ACTOR AND THE ALIBI

MR. MUNDON MANDEVILLE, the theatrical manager, walked briskly through the passages behind the scenes, or rather below the scenes. His attire was smart and festive, perhaps a little too festive; the flower in his buttonhole was festive; the very varnish on his boots was festive; but his face was not at all festive. He was a big, bull-necked, black- browed man, and at the moment his brow was blacker than usual. He had in any case, of course, the hundred botherations that besiege a man in such a position; and they ranged from large to small and from new to old. It annoyed him to pass through the passages where the old pantomime scenery was stacked; because he had successfully begun, his career at that theatre with very popular pantomimes, and had since been induced to gamble in more serious and classical drama over which he had dropped a good deal of money. Hence, to see the sapphire Gates of Bluebeard's Blue Palace, or portions of the Enchanted Grove of Golden Orange Trees, leaning up against the wall to be festooned with cobwebs or nibbled by mice, did not give him that soothing sense of a return to simplicity which we all ought to have when given a glimpse of that wonderland of our childhood. Nor had he any time to drop a tear where he had dropped the money, or to dream of this Paradise of Peter Pan; for he had been summoned hurriedly to settle a practical problem, not of the past but of the moment. It was the sort of thing that does sometimes happen in that strange world behind the scenes; but it was big enough to be serious. Miss Maroni, the talented young actress of Italian parentage, who had undertaken to act an important part in the play that was to be rehearsed that afternoon and performed that evening, had abruptly and even violently refused at the last moment to do anything of the kind. He had not even seen the exasperating lady yet; and as she had locked herself up in her dressing-room and defied the world through the door, it seemed unlikely, for the present, that he would. Mr. Mundon Mandeville was sufficiently British to explain it by murmuring that all foreigners were mad; but the thought of his good fortune in inhabiting the only sane island of the planet did not suffice to soothe him any more than the memory of the Enchanted Grove. All these things, and many more, were annoying; and yet a very intimate observer might have suspected that something was wrong with Mr. Mandeville that went beyond annoyance.

If it be possible for a heavy and healthy man to look haggard, he looked haggard. His face was full, but his eye-sockets were hollow; his mouth twitched as if it were always trying to bite the black strip of moustache that was just too short to be bitten. He might have been a man who had begun to take drugs; but even on that assumption there was something that suggested that he had a reason for doing it; that the drug was not the cause of the tragedy, but the tragedy the cause of the drug. Whatever was his deeper secret, it seemed to inhabit that dark end of the long passage where was the entrance to his own little study; and as he went along the empty corridor, he threw back a nervous glance now and then.

However, business is business; and he made his way to the opposite end of the passage where the blank green door of Miss Maroni defied the world. A group of actors and other people involved were already standing in front of it, conferring and considering, one might almost fancy, the advisability of a battering-ram. The group contained one figure, at least, who was already well enough known; whose photograph was on many mantelpieces and his autograph in many albums. For though Norman Knight was playing the hero in a theatre that was still a little provincial and old-fashioned and capable of calling him the first walking gentleman, he, at least, was certainly on the way to wider triumphs. He was a good - looking man with a long cleft chin and fair hair low on his forehead, giving him a rather Neronian look that did not altogether correspond to his impulsive and plunging movements. The group also contained Ralph Randall, who generally acted elderly character parts, and had a humorous hatchet face, blue with shaving, and discoloured with grease paint. It contained Mandeville's second walking gentleman, carrying on the not yet wholly vanished tradition of Charles's Friend, a dark, curly-haired youth of somewhat Semitic profile bearing the name of Aubrey Vernon.

It included Mr. Mundon Mandeville's wife's maid or dresser, a very powerful-looking person with tight red hair and a hard wooden face. It also, incidentally, included Mandeville's wife, a quiet woman in the background, with a pale, patient face, the lines of which had not lost a classical symmetry and severity, but which looked all the paler because her very eyes were pale, and her pale yellow hair lay in two plain bands like some very archaic Madonna. Not everybody knew that she had once been a serious and successful actress in Ibsen and the intellectual drama. But her husband did not think much of problem plays; and certainly at the moment was more interested in the problem of getting a foreign actress out of a locked room; a new version of the conjuring trick of the Vanishing Lady.

"Hasn't she come out yet?" he demanded, speaking to his wife's business -like attendant rather than to his wife.

"No, sir," answered the woman — who was known as Mrs. Sands — in a sombre manner.

"We are beginning to get a little alarmed," said old Randall. "She seemed quite unbalanced, and we're afraid she might even do herself some mischief."

"Hell!" said Mandeville in his simple and artless way. "Advertisement's very good, but we don't want that sort of advertisement. Hasn't she any friends here? Has nobody any influence with her?"

"Jarvis thinks the only man who might manage her is her own priest round the corner," said Randall; "and in case she does start hanging herself on a hat peg, I really thought perhaps he'd better be here. Jarvis has gone to fetch him and, as a matter of fact, here he comes."

Two more figures appeared in that subterranean passage under the stage: the first was Ashton Jarvis, a jolly fellow who generally acted villains, but who had surrendered that high vocation for the moment to the curly-headed youth with the nose. The other figure was short and square and clad all in black; it was Father Brown from the church round the corner.

Father Brown seemed to take it quite naturally and even casually, that he should be called in to consider the queer conduct of one of his flock, whether she was to be regarded as a black sheep or only as a lost lamb. But he did not seem to think much of the suggestion of suicide.

"I suppose there was some reason for her flying off the handle like that," he said. "Does anybody know what it was?"

"Dissatisfied with her part, I believe," said the older actor.

"They always are," growled Mr. Mundon Mandeville. "And I thought my wife would look after those arrangements."

"I can only say," said Mrs. Mundon Mandeville rather wearily, "that I gave her what ought to be the best part. It's supposed to be what stage - struck young women want, isn't it — to act the beautiful young heroine and marry the beautiful young hero in a shower of bouquets and cheers from the gallery? Women of my age naturally have to fall back on acting respectable matrons, and I was careful to confine myself to that."

"It would be devilish awkward to alter the parts now, anyhow," said Randall.

"It's not to be thought of," declared Norman Knight firmly. "Why, I could hardly act — but anyhow it's much too late."

Father Brown had slipped forward and was standing outside the locked door listening.

"Is there no sound?" asked the manager anxiously; and then added in a lower voice: "Do you think she can have done herself in?"

"There is a certain sound," replied Father Brown calmly. "I should be inclined to deduce from the sound that she is engaged in breaking windows or looking-glasses, probably with her feet. No; I do not think there is much danger of her going on to destroy herself. Breaking looking-glasses with your feet is a very unusual prelude to suicide. If she had been a German, gone away to think quietly about metaphysics and weltschmerz, I should be all for breaking the door down. These Italians don't really die so easily; and are not liable to kill themselves in a rage. Somebody else, perhaps-yes, possibly-it might be well to take ordinary precautions if she comes out with a leap."

"So you're not in favour of forcing the door?" asked Mandeville.

"Not if you want her to act in your play," replied Father Brown. "If you do that, she'll raise the roof and refuse to stay in the place; if you leave her alone-she'll probably come out from mere curiosity. If I were you, I should just leave somebody to guard the door, more or less, and trust to time for an hour or two."

"In that case," said Mandeville, "we can only get on with rehearsing the scenes where she doesn't appear. My wife will arrange all that is necessary for scenery just now. After all, the fourth act is the main business. You had better get on with that."

"Not a dress rehearsal," said Mandeville's wife to the others.

"Very well," said Knight, "not a dress rehearsal, of course. I wish the dresses of the infernal period weren't so elaborate."

"What is the play?" asked the priest with a touch of curiosity.

"The School for Scandal," said Mandeville. "It may be literature, but I want plays. My wife likes what she calls classical comedies. A long sight more classic than comic."

At this moment, the old doorkeeper known as Sam, and the solitary inhabitant of the theatre during off-hours, came waddling up to the manager with a card, to say that Lady Miriam Marden wished to see him. He turned away, but Father Brown continued to blink steadily for a few seconds in the direction of the manager's wife, and saw that her wan face wore a faint smile; not altogether a cheerful smile.

Father Brown moved off in company with the man who had brought him in, who happened, indeed, to be a friend and person of a similar persuasion, which is not uncommon among actors. As he moved off, however, he heard Mrs. Mandeville give quiet directions to Mrs. Sands that she should take up the post of watcher beside the closed door.

"Mrs. Mandeville seems to be an intelligent woman," said the priest to his companion, "though she keeps so much in the background."

"She was once a highly intellectual woman," said Jarvis sadly; "rather washed-out and wasted, some would say, by marrying a bounder like Mandeville. She has the very highest ideals of the drama, you know; but, of course, it isn't often she can get her lord and master to look at anything in that light. Do you know, he actually wanted a woman like that to act as a pantomime boy? Admitted that she was a fine actress, but said pantomimes paid better. That will give you about a measure of his psychological insight and sensibility. But she never complained. As she said to me once: 'Complaint always comes back in an echo from the ends of the world; but silence strengthens us.' If only she were married to somebody who understood her ideas she might have been one of the great actresses of the age; indeed, the highbrow critics still think a lot of her. As it is, she is married to that."

And he pointed to where the big black bulk of Mandeville stood with his back to them, talking to the ladies who had summoned him forth into the vestibule. Lady Miriam was a very long and languid and elegant lady, handsome in a recent fashion largely modelled on Egyptian mummies; her dark hair cut low and square, like a sort of helmet, and her lips very painted and prominent and giving her a permanent expression of contempt. Her companion was a very vivacious lady with an ugly attractive face and hair powdered with grey. She was a Miss Theresa Talbot and she talked a great deal, while her companion seemed too tired to talk at all. Only, just as the two men passed. Lady Miriam summoned up the energy to say:

"Plays are a bore; but I've never seen a rehearsal in ordinary clothes. Might be a bit funny. Somehow, nowadays, one can never find a thing one's never seen."

"Now, Mr. Mandeville," said Miss Talbot, tapping him on the arm with animated persistence, "you simply must let us see that rehearsal. We can't come to-night, and we don't want to. We want to see all the funny people in the wrong clothes."

"Of course I can give you a box if you wish it," said Mandeville hastily. "Perhaps your ladyship would come this way." And he led them off down another corridor.

"I wonder," said Jarvis in a meditative manner, "whether even Mandeville prefers that sort of woman."

"Well," asked his clerical companion, "have you any reason to suppose that Mandeville does prefer her?"

Jarvis looked at him steadily for an instant before answering.

"Mandeville is a mystery," he said gravely. "Oh, yes, I know that he looks about as commonplace a cad as ever walked down Piccadilly. But he really is a mystery for all that. There's something on his conscience. There's a shadow in his life. And I doubt whether it has anything more to do with a few fashionable flirtations than it has with his poor neglected wife. If it has, there's something more in them than meets the eye. As a matter of fact, I happen to know rather more about it than anyone else does, merely by accident. But even I can't make anything of what I know, except a mystery."

He looked around him in the vestibule to see that they were alone and then added, lowering his voice:

"I don't mind telling you, because I know you are a tower of silence where secrets are concerned. But I had a curious shock the other day; and it has been repeated several times since. You know that Mandeville always works in that little room at the end of the passage, just under the stage. Well, twice over I happened to pass by there when everyone thought he was alone; and what's more, when I myself happened to be able to account for all the women in the company, and all the women likely to have to do with him, being absent or at their usual posts."

"All the women?" remarked Father Brown inquiringly.

"There was a woman with him," said Jarvis almost in a whisper. "There is some woman who is always visiting him; somebody that none of us knows. I don't even know how she comes there, since it isn't down the passage to the door; but I think I once saw a veiled or cloaked figure passing out into the twilight at the back of the theatre, like a ghost. But she can't be a ghost. And I don't believe she's even an ordinary 'affair'. I don't think it's love-making. I think it's blackmail."

"What makes you think that?" asked the other.

"Because," said Jarvis, his face turning from grave to grim, "I once heard sounds like a quarrel; and then the strange woman said in a metallic, menacing voice, four words: 'I am your wife.'"

"You think he's a bigamist," said Father Brown reflectively. "Well, bigamy and blackmail often go together, of course. But she may be bluffing as well as blackmailing. She may be mad. These theatrical people often have monomaniacs running after them. You may be right, but I shouldn't jump to conclusions. . . . And talking about theatrical people, isn't the rehearsal going to begin, and aren't you a theatrical person?"

"I'm not on in this scene," said Jarvis with a smile. "They're only doing one act, you know, until your Italian friend comes to her senses."

"Talking about my Italian friend," observed the priest, "I should rather like to know whether she has come to her senses."

"We can go back and see, if you like," said Jarvis; and they descended again to the basement and the long passage, at one end of which was Mandeville's study and at the other the closed door of Signora Maroni. The door seemed to be still closed; and. Mrs. Sands sat grimly outside it, as motionless as a wooden idol.

Near the other end of the passage they caught a glimpse of some of the other actors in the scene mounting the stairs to the stage just above. Vernon and old Randall went ahead, running rapidly up the stairs; but Mrs. Mandeville went more slowly, in her quietly dignified fashion, and

Norman Knight seemed to linger a little to speak to her. A few words fell on the ears of the unintentional eavesdroppers as they passed.

"I tell you a woman visits him," Knight was saying violently.

"Hush!" said the lady in her voice of silver that still had in it something of steel. "You must not talk like this. Remember, he is my husband."

"I wish to God I could forget it," said Knight, and rushed up the stairs to the stage.

The lady followed him, still pale and calm, to take up her own position there.

"Somebody else knows it," said the priest quietly; "but I doubt whether it is any business of ours."

"Yes," muttered Jarvis; "it seems as if everybody knows it and nobody knows anything about it."

They proceeded along the passage to the other end, where the rigid attendant sat outside the Italian's door.

"No; she ain't come out yet," said the woman in her sullen way; "and she ain't dead, for I heard her moving about now and then. I dunno what tricks she's up to."

"Do you happen to know, ma'am," said Father Brown with abrupt politeness, "where Mr. Mandeville is just now?"

"Yes," she replied promptly. "Saw him go into his little room at the end of the passage a minute or two ago; just before the prompter called and the curtain went up-Must be there still, for I ain't seen him come out."

"There's no other door to his office, you mean," said Father Brown in an off-hand way. "Well, I suppose the rehearsal's going in full swing now, for all the Signora's sulking."

"Yes," said Jarvis after a moment's silence; "I can just hear the voices on the stage from here. Old Randall has a splendid carrying voice."

They both remained for an instant in a listening attitude, so that the booming voice of the actor on the stage could indeed be heard rolling faintly down the stairs and along the passage. Before they had spoken again or resumed their normal poise, their ears were filled with another sound. It was a dull but heavy crash and it came from behind the closed door of Mundon Mandeville's private room.

Father Brown went racing along the passage like an arrow from the bow and was struggling with the door-handle before Jarvis had wakened with a start and begun to follow him.

"The door is locked," said the priest, turning a face that was a little pale. "And I am all in favour of breaking down this door."

"Do you mean," asked Jarvis with a rather ghastly look, "that the unknown visitor has got in here again? Do you think it's anything serious?" After a moment he added: "I may be able to push back the bolt; I know the fastening on these doors."

He knelt down and pulled out a pocket-knife with a long steel implement, manipulated it for a moment, and the door swung open on the manager's study. Almost the first thing they noticed was that there was no other door and even no window, but a great electric lamp stood on the table. But it was not quite the first thing that they noticed; for even before that they had seen that Mandeville was lying flat on his face in the middle of the room and the blood was crawling out from under his fallen face like a pattern of scarlet snakes that glittered evilly in that unnatural subterranean light.

They did not know how long they had been staring at each other when Jarvis said, like one letting loose something that he had held back with his breath:

"If the stranger got in somehow, she has gone somehow."

"Perhaps we think too much about the stranger," said Father Brown. "There are so many strange things in this strange theatre that you rather tend to forget some of them."

"Why, which things do you mean?" asked his friend quickly.

"There are many," said the priest. "There is the other locked door, for instance."

"But the other door is locked," cried Jarvis staring.

"But you forgot it all the same," said Father Brown. A few moments afterwards he said thoughtfully: "That Mrs. Sands is a grumpy and gloomy sort of card."

"Do you mean," asked the other in a lowered voice, "that she's lying and the Italian did come out?"

"No," said the priest calmly; "I think I meant it more or less as a detached study of character."

"You can't mean," cried the actor, "that Mrs. Sands did it herself?"

"I didn't mean a study of her character," said Father Brown.

While they had been exchanging these abrupt reflections, Father Brown had knelt down by the body and ascertained that it was beyond any hope or question a dead body. Lying beside it, though not immediately visible from the doorway, was a dagger of the theatrical sort; lying as if it had fallen from the wound or from the hand of the assassin. According to Jarvis, who recognized the instrument, there was not very much to be learned from it, unless the experts could find some finger-prints. It was a property dagger; that is, it was nobody's property; it had been kicking about the theatre for a long time, and anybody might have picked it up. Then the priest rose and looked gravely round the room.

"We must send for the police," he said; "and for a doctor, though the doctor comes too late. Looking at this room, by the way, I don't see how our Italian friend could manage it."

"The Italian!" cried his friend; "I should think not. I should have thought she had an alibi, if anybody had. Two separate rooms, both locked, at opposite ends of a long passage, with a fixed witness watching it."

"No," said Father Brown. "Not quite. The difficulty is how she could have got in this end. I think she might have got out the other end."

"And why?" asked the other.

"I told you," said Father Brown, "that it sounded as if she was breaking glass—mirrors or windows. Stupidly enough I forgot something I knew quite well; that she is pretty superstitious. She wouldn't be likely to break a mirror; so I suspect she broke a window. It's true that all this is under the ground floor; but it might be a skylight or a window opening on an area. But there don't seem to be any skylights or areas here." And he stared at the ceiling very intently for a considerable time.

Suddenly he came back to conscious life again with a start. "We must go upstairs and telephone and tell everybody, It is pretty painful ... My God, can you hear those actors still shouting and ranting upstairs? The play is still going on. I suppose that's what they mean by tragic irony."

When it was fated that the theatre should be turned into a house of mourning, an opportunity was given to the actors to show many of the real virtues of their type and trade. They did, as the phrase goes, behave like gentlemen; and not only like first walking gentlemen. They had not all of them liked or trusted Mandeville, but they knew exactly the right things to say about him; they showed not only sympathy but delicacy in their attitude to his widow. She had become, in a new and very different sense, a tragedy queen—her lightest word was law and while she moved about slowly and sadly, they ran her many errands.

"She was always a strong character," said old Randall rather huskily; "and had the best brains of any of us. Of course poor Mandeville was never on her level in education and so on; but she always did her duty splendidly. It was quite pathetic the way she would sometimes say she wished she had more intellectual life; but Mandeville—well, nil nisi bonum, as they say." And the old gentleman went away wagging his head sadly.

"Nil nisi bonum indeed," said Jarvis grimly. "I don't think Randall at any rate has heard of the story of the strange lady visitor. By the way, don't you think it probably was the strange woman?"

"It depends," said the priest, "whom you mean by the strange woman."

"Oh! I don't mean the Italian woman," said Jarvis hastily. "Though, as a matter of fact, you were quite right about her, too. When they went in the skylight was smashed and the room was empty; but so far as the police can discover, she simply went home in the most harmless fashion. No, I mean the woman who was heard threatening him at that secret meeting; the woman who said she was his wife. Do you think she really was his wife?"

"It is possible," said Father Brown, staring blankly into the void, "that she really was his wife."

"That would give us the motive of jealousy over his bigamous remarriage," reflected Jarvis, "for the body was not robbed in any way. No need to poke about for thieving servants or even impecunious actors. But as for that, of course, you've noticed the outstanding and peculiar thing about the case?"

"I have noticed several peculiar things," said Father Brown. "Which one do you mean?"

"I mean the corporate alibi," said Jarvis gravely. "It's not often that practically a whole company has a public alibi like that; an alibi on a lighted stage and all witnessing to each other. As it turns out it is jolly lucky for our friends here that poor Mandeville did put those two silly society women in the box to watch the rehearsal. They can bear witness that the whole act was performed without a hitch, with the characters on the stage all the time. They began long before Mandeville was last seen going into his room. They went on at least five or ten minutes after you and I found his dead body. And, by a lucky coincidence, the moment we actually heard him fall was during the time when all the characters were on the stage together."

"Yes, that is certainly very important and simplifies everything," agreed Father Brown. "Let us count the people covered by the alibi. There was Randall: I rather fancy Randall practically hated the manager, though he is very properly covering his feelings just now. But he is ruled out; it was his voice we heard thundering over our heads from the stage. There is our jeune premier, Mr. Knight: I have rather good reason to suppose he was in love with Mandeville's wife and not concealing that sentiment so much as he might; but he is out of it, for he was on the stage at the same time, being thundered at. There was that amiable Jew who calls himself Aubrey Vernon, he's out of it; and there's Mrs. Mandeville, she's out of it. Their corporate alibi, as you say, depends chiefly on Lady Miriam and her friend in the box; though there is the general common-sense corroboration that the act had to be gone through and the routine of the theatre seems to have suffered no interruption. The legal witnesses, however, are Lady Miriam and her friend, Miss Talbot. I suppose you feel sure they are all right?"

"Lady Miriam?" said Jarvis in surprise. "Oh, yes. ... I suppose you mean that she looks a queer sort of vamp. But you've no notion what even the ladies of the best families are looking like nowadays. Besides, is there any particular reason for doubting their evidence?"

"Only that it brings us up against a blank wall," said Father Brown. "Don't you see that this collective alibi practically covers everybody? Those four were the only performers in the theatre at the time; and there were scarcely any servants in the theatre; none indeed, except old Sam, who guards the only regular entrance, and the woman who guarded Miss Maroni's door. There is nobody else left available but you and me. We certainly might be accused of the crime, especially as we found the body. There seems nobody else who can be accused. You didn't happen to kill him when I wasn't looking, I suppose?"

Jarvis looked up with a slight start and stared a moment, then the broad grin returned to his swarthy face. He shook his head.

"You didn't do it," said Father Brown; "and we will assume for the moment, merely for the sake of argument, that I didn't do it. The people on the stage being out of it, it really leaves the Signora behind her locked door, the sentinel in front other door, and old Sam. Or are you thinking of the two ladies in the box? Of course they might have slipped out of the box."

"No," said Jarvis; "I am thinking of the unknown woman who came and told Mandeville she was his wife."

"Perhaps she was," said the priest; and this time there was a note in his steady voice that made his companion start to his feet once more and lean across the table.

"We said," he observed in a low, eager voice, "that this first wife might have been jealous of the other wife."

"No," said Father Brown; "she might have been jealous of the Italian girl, perhaps, or of Lady Miriam Marden. But she was not jealous of the other wife."

"And why not?"

"Because there was no other wife," said Father Brown. "So far from being a bigamist, Mr. Mandeville seems to me to have been a highly monogamous person. His wife was almost too much with him; so much with him that you all charitably suppose that she must be somebody else. But I don't see how she could have been with him when he was killed, for we agree that she was acting all the time in front of the footlights. Acting an important part, too. ..."

"Do you really mean," cried Jarvis, "that the strange woman who haunted him like a ghost was only the Mrs. Mandeville we know?" But he received no answer; for Father Brown was staring into vacancy with a blank expression almost like an idiot's. He always did look most idiotic at the instant when he was most intelligent.

The next moment he scrambled to his feet, looking very harassed and distressed. "This is awful," he said. "I'm not sure it isn't the worst business I ever had; but I've got to go through with it. Would you go and ask Mrs. Mandeville if I may speak to her in private?"

"Oh, certainly," said Jarvis, as he turned towards the door. "But what's the matter with you?"

"Only being a born fool," said Father Brown; "a very common complaint in this vale of tears. I was fool enough to forget altogether that the play was The School for Scandal."

He walked restlessly up and down the room until Jarvis re-appeared at the door with an altered and even alarmed face.

"I can't find her anywhere," he said. "Nobody seems to have seen her."

"They haven't seen Norman Knight either, have they?" asked Father Brown dryly. "Well, it saves me the most painful interview of my life. Saving the grace of God, I was very nearly frightened of that woman. But she was frightened of me, too; frightened of something I'd seen or said. Knight was always begging her to bolt with him. Now she's done it; and I'm devilish sorry for him."

"For him?" inquired Jarvis.

"Well, it can't be very nice to elope with a murderess," said the other dispassionately. "But as a matter of fact she was something very much worse than a murderess."

"And what is that?"

"An egoist," said Father Brown. "She was the sort of person who had looked in the mirror before looking out of the window, and it is the worst calamity of mortal life. The looking-glass was unlucky for her, all right; but rather because it wasn't broken."

"I can't understand what all this means," said Jarvis. "Everybody regarded her as a person of the most exalted ideals, almost moving on a higher spiritual plane than the rest of us. ..."

"She regarded herself in that light," said the other; "and she knew how to hypnotize everybody else into it. Perhaps I hadn't known her long enough to be wrong about her. But I knew the sort of person she was five minutes after I clapped eyes on her."

"Oh, come." cried Jarvis; "I'm sure her behaviour about the Italian was beautiful."

"Her behaviour always was beautiful," said the other. "I've heard from everybody here all about her refinements and subtleties and spiritual soarings above poor Mandeville's head. But all these spiritualities and subtleties seem to me to boil themselves clown to the simple fact that she certainly was a lady and he most certainly was not a gentleman. But, do you know, I have never felt quite sure that St. Peter will make that the only test at the gate of heaven.

"As for the rest," he went on with increasing animation, "I knew from the very first words she said that she was not really being fair to the poor Italian, with all her fine airs of frigid magnanimity. And again, I realized it when I knew that the play was The School for Scandal.'

"You are going rather too fast for me," said Jarvis in some bewilderment. "What does it matter what the play was?"

"Well," said the priest, "she said she had given the girl the part of the beautiful heroine and had retired into the background herself with the older part of a matron. Now that might have applied to almost any play; but it falsifies the facts about that particular play. She can only have meant that she gave the other actress the part of Maria, which is hardly a part at all. And the part of the obscure and self-effacing married woman, if you please, must have been the part of Lady Teazle, which is the only part any actress wants to act. If the Italian was a first-rate actress who had been promised a first-rate part, there was really some excuse, or at least some cause, for her mad Italian rage. There generally is for mad Italian rages: Latins are logical and have a reason for going mad. But that one little thing let in daylight for me on the meaning of her magnanimity. And there was another thing, even then. You laughed when I said that the sulky look of Mrs. Sands was a study in character; but not in the character of Mrs. Sands. But it was true. If you want to know what a lady is really like, don't look at her; for she may be too clever for you. Don't look at the men round her, for they may be too silly about her. But look at some other woman who is always near to her, and especially one who is under her. You will see in that mirror her real face, and the face mirrored in Mrs. Sands was very ugly.

"And as for all the other impressions, what were they? I heard a lot about the unworthiness of poor old Mandeville; but it was all about his being unworthy other, and I am pretty certain it came indirectly from her. And, even so, it betrayed itself. Obviously, from what every man said, she had confided in every man about her confounded intellectual loneliness. You yourself said she never complained; and then quoted her about how her uncomplaining silence strengthened her soul. And that is just the note; that's the unmistakable style. People who complain are just jolly, human

Christian nuisances; I don't mind them. But people who complain that they never complain are the devil. They are really the devil; isn't that swagger of stoicism the whole point of the Byronic cult of Satan? I heard all this; but for the life of me I couldn't hear of anything tangible she had to complain of. Nobody pretended that her husband drank, or beat her, or left her without money, or even was unfaithful, until the rumour about the secret meetings, which were simply her own melodramatic habit of pestering him with curtain- lectures in his own business office. And when one looked at the facts, apart from the atmospheric impression of martyrdom she contrived to spread, the facts were really quite the other way. Mandeville left off making money on pantomimes to please her; he started losing money on classical drama to please her. She arranged the scenery and furniture as she liked. She wanted Sheridan's play and she had it; she wanted the part of Lady Teazle and she had it; she wanted a rehearsal without costume at that particular hour and she had it. It may be worth remarking on the curious fact that she wanted that."

"But what is the use of all this tirade?" asked the actor, who had hardly ever heard his clerical friend, make so long a speech before. "We seem to have got a long way from the murder in all this psychological business. She may have eloped with Knight; she may have bamboozled Randall; she may have bamboozled me. But she can't have murdered her husband — for everyone agrees she was on the stage through the whole scene. She may be wicked; but she isn't a witch."

"Well, I wouldn't be so sure," said Father Brown, with a smile. "But she didn't need to use any witchcraft in this case. I know now that she did it, and very simply indeed."

"Why are you so sure of that?" asked Jarvis, looking at him in a puzzled way.

"Because the play was The School for Scandal," replied Father Brown, "and that particular act of The School for Scandal. I should like to remind you, as I said just now, that she always arranged the furniture how she liked. I should also like to remind you that this stage was built and used for pantomimes; it would naturally have trap-doors and trick exits of that sort. And when you say that witnesses could attest to having seen all the performers on the stage, I should like to remind you that in the principal scene of The School for Scandal one of the principal performers remains for a considerable time on the stage, but is not seen. She is technically 'on,' but she might practically be very much 'off.' That is the Screen of Lady Teazle and the Alibi of Mrs. Mandeville."

There was a silence and then the actor said: "You think she slipped through a trap-door behind a screen down to the floor below, where the manager's room was?"

"She certainly slipped away in some fashion; and that is the most probable fashion," said the other. "I think it all the more probable because she took the opportunity of an undress rehearsal, and even indeed arranged for one. It is a guess; but I fancy if it had been a dress rehearsal it might have been more difficult to get through a trap -door in the hoops of the eighteenth century. There are many little difficulties, of course, but I think they could all be met in time and in turn."

"What I can't meet is the big difficulty," said Jarvis, putting his head on his hand with a sort of groan. "I simply can't bring myself to believe that a radiant and serene creature like that could so lose, so to speak, her bodily balance, to say nothing of her moral balance. Was any motive strong enough? Was she very much in love with Knight?"

"I hope so," replied his companion; "for really it would be the most human excuse. But I'm sorry to say that I have my doubts. She wanted to get rid of her husband, who was an old-fashioned, provincial hack, not even making much money. She wanted to have a career as the brilliant wife of a brilliant and rapidly-rising actor. But she didn't want in that sense to act in The School for Scandal. She wouldn't have run away with a man except in the last resort. It wasn't a human passion with her, but a sort of hellish respectability. She was always dogging her husband in secret and badgering him to divorce himself or otherwise get out of the way; and as he refused he paid at last for his refusal. There's another thing you've got to remember. You talk about these highbrows having a higher art and a more philosophical drama. But remember what a lot of the philosophy is! Remember what sort of conduct those highbrows often present to the highest! All about the Will to Power and the Right to Live and the Right to Experience-damned nonsense and more than damned nonsense – nonsense that can damn."

Father Brown frowned, which he did very rarely; and there was still a cloud on his brow as he put on his hat and went out into the night.

VI: THE VANISHING OF VAUDREY

SIR ARTHUR VAUDREY, in his light-grey summer suit, and wearing on his grey head the white hat which he so boldly affected, went walking briskly up the road by the river from his own house to the little group of houses that were almost like outhouses to his own, entered that little hamlet, and then vanished completely as if he had been carried away by the fairies.

The disappearance seemed the more absolute and abrupt because of the familiarity of the scene and the extreme simplicity of the conditions of the problem. The hamlet could not be called a village; indeed, it was little more than a small and strangely-isolated street. It stood in the middle of wide and open fields and plains, a mere string of the four or five shops absolutely needed by the neighbours; that is, by a few farmers and the family at the great house. There was a butcher's at the corner, at which, it appeared, Sir Arthur had last been seen. He was seen by two young men staying at his house—Evan Smith, who was acting as his secretary, and John Dalmon, who was generally supposed to be engaged to his ward. There was next to the butcher's a small shop combining a large number of functions, such as is found in villages, in which a little old woman sold sweets, walking-sticks, golf-balls, gum, balls of string and a very faded sort of stationery. Beyond this was the tobacconist, to which the two young men were betaking themselves when they last caught a glimpse of their host standing in front of the butcher's shop; and beyond that was a dingy little dressmaker's, kept by two ladies. A pale and shiny shop, offering to the passer-by great goblets of very wan, green lemonade, completed the block of buildings; for the only real and Christian inn in the neighbourhood stood by itself some way, down the main road. Between the inn and the hamlet was a cross-roads, at which stood a policeman and a uniformed official of a motoring club; and both agreed that Sir Arthur had never passed that point on the road.

It had been at an early hour of a very brilliant summer day that the old gentleman had gone gaily striding up the road, swinging his walking-stick and flapping his yellow gloves. He was a good deal of a dandy, but one of a vigorous and virile sort, especially for his age. His bodily strength and activity were still very remarkable, and his curly hair might have been a yellow so pale as to look white instead of a white that was a faded yellow. His clean-shaven face was handsome, with a high-bridged nose like the Duke of Wellington's; but the most outstanding features were his eyes. They were not merely metaphorically outstanding; something prominent and almost bulging about them was perhaps the only disproportion in his features; but his lips were sensitive and set a little tightly, as if by an act of will. He was the squire of all that country and the owner of the little hamlet. In that sort of place everybody not only knows everybody else, but generally knows where anybody is at any given moment. The normal course would have been for Sir Arthur to walk to the village, to say whatever he wanted to say to the butcher or anybody else, and then walk back to his house again, all in the course of about half an hour: as the two young men did when they had bought their cigarettes. But they saw nobody on the road returning; indeed, there was nobody in sight except the one other guest at the house, a certain Dr. Abbott, who was sitting with his broad back to them on the river bank, very patiently fishing.

When all the three guests returned to breakfast, they seemed to think little or nothing of the continued absence of the squire; but when the day wore on and he missed one meal after another, they naturally began to be puzzled, and Sybil Rye, the lady of the household, began to be seriously alarmed. Expeditions of discovery were dispatched to the village again and again without finding any trace; and eventually, when darkness fell, the house was full of a definite fear. Sybil had sent for Father Brown, who was a friend of hers and had helped her out of a difficulty in the past; and under the pressure of the apparent peril he had consented to remain at the house and see it through.

Thus it happened that when the new day's dawn broke without news, Father Brown was early afoot and on the look-out for anything; his black, stumpy figure could be seen pacing the garden path where the garden was embanked along the river, as he scanned the landscape up and down with his short-sighted and rather misty gaze.

He realized that another figure was moving even more restlessly along the embankment, and saluted Evan Smith, the secretary, by name.

Evan Smith was a tall, fair-haired young man, looking rather harassed, as was perhaps natural in that hour of distraction. But something of the sort hung about him at all times. Perhaps it was more marked because he had the sort of athletic reach and poise and the sort of leonine yellow hair and moustache which accompany (always in fiction and sometimes in fact) a frank and cheerful demeanour of "English youth." As in his case they accompanied deep and cavernous eyes and a rather haggard look, the contrast with the conventional tall figure and fair hair of romance may have had a touch of something sinister. But Father Brown smiled at him amiably enough and then said more seriously:

"This is a trying business."

"It's a very trying business for Miss Rye," answered the young man gloomily; "and I don't see why I should disguise what's the worst part of it for me, even if she is engaged to Dalmon. Shocked, I suppose?"

Father Brown did not look very much shocked, but his face was often rather expressionless; he merely said, mildly:

"Naturally, we all sympathize with her anxiety. I suppose you haven't any news or views in the matter?"

"I haven't any news exactly." answered Smith; "no news from outside at least. As for views. ..." And he relapsed into moody silence.

"I should be very glad to hear your views," said the little priest pleasantly. "I hope you don't mind my saying that you seem to have something on your mind."

The young man stirred rather than started and looked at the priest steadily, with a frown that threw his hollow eyes into dense shadow.

"Well, you're right enough," he said at last. "I suppose I shall have to tell somebody. And you seem a safe sort of person to tell."

"Do you know what has happened to Sir Arthur?" asked Father Brown calmly, as if it were the most casual matter in the world.

"Yes," said the secretary harshly, "I think I know what has happened to Sir Arthur."

"A beautiful morning," said a bland voice in his ear; "a beautiful morning for a rather melancholy meeting."

This time the secretary jumped as if he had been shot, as the large shadow of Dr. Abbott fell across his path in the already strong sunshine. Dr. Abbott was still in his dressing-gown—a sumptuous oriental dressing-gown covered with coloured flowers and dragons, looking rather like one of the most brilliant flower-beds that were growing under the glowing sun. He also wore large, flat slippers, which was doubtless why he had come so close to the others without being heard. He would normally have seemed the last person for such a light and airy approach, for he was a very big, broad and heavy man, with a powerful benevolent face very much sunburnt, in a frame of old- fashioned grey whiskers and chin beard, which hung about him luxuriantly, like the long, grey curls of his venerable head. His long slits of eyes were rather sleepy and, indeed, he was an elderly gentleman to be up so early; but he had a look at once robust and weather-beaten, as of an old farmer or sea captain who had once been out in all weathers. He was the only old comrade and contemporary of the squire in the company that met at the house.

"It seems truly extraordinary," he said, shaking his head. "Those little houses are like dolls' houses, always open front and back, and there's hardly room to hide anybody, even if they wanted to hide him. And I'm sure they don't. Dalmon and I cross-examined them all yesterday; they're mostly little old women that couldn't hurt a fly. The men are nearly all away harvesting, except the butcher; and Arthur was seen coining out of the butcher's. And nothing could have happened along that stretch by the river, for I was fishing there all day."

Then he looked at Smith and the look in his long eyes seemed for the moment not only sleepy, but a little sly.

"I think you and Dalmon can testify," he said, "that you saw me sitting there through your whole journey there and back."

"Yes," said Evan Smith shortly, and seemed rather impatient at the long interruption.

"The only thing I can think of," went on Dr. Abbott slowly; and then the interruption was itself interrupted. A figure at once light and sturdy strode very rapidly across the green lawn between the gay flowerbeds, and John Dalmon appeared among them, holding a paper in his hand. He was neatly dressed and rather swarthy, with a very fine square Napoleonic face and very sad eyes — eyes so sad that they looked almost dead. He seemed to be still young, but his black hair had gone prematurely grey about the temples.

"I've just had this telegram from the police," he said "I wired to them last night and they say they're sending down a man at once. Do you know, Dr. Abbott, of anybody else we ought to send for? Relations, I mean, and that sort of thing."

"There is his nephew, Vernon Vaudrey, of course," said the old man. "If you will come with me, I think I can give you his address and — and tell you something rather special about him."

Dr. Abbott and Dalmon moved away in the direction of the house and, when they had gone a certain distance, Father Brown said simply, as if there had been no interruption:

"You were saying?"

"You're a cool hand," said the secretary. "I suppose it comes of hearing confessions. I feel rather as if I were going to make a confession. Some people would feel a bit jolted out of the mood of confidence by that queer old elephant creeping up like a snake. But I suppose I'd better stick to it, though it really isn't my confession, but somebody else's." He stopped a moment, frowning and pulling his moustache; then he said, abruptly:

"I believe Sir Arthur has bolted, and I believe I know why."

There was a silence and then he exploded again.

"I'm in a damnable position, and most people would say I was doing a damnable thing. I am now going to appear in the character of a sneak and a skunk and I believe I am doing my duty."

"You must be the judge," said Father Brown gravely. "What is the matter with your duty?"

"I'm in the perfectly foul position of telling tales against a rival, and a successful rival, too," said the young man bitterly; "and I don't know what else in the world I can do. You were asking what was the explanation of Vaudrey's disappearance. I am absolutely convinced that Dalmon is the explanation."

"You mean," said the priest, with composure, "that Dalmon has killed Sir Arthur?"

"No!" exploded Smith, with startling violence. "No, a hundred times! He hasn't done that, whatever else he's done. He isn't a murderer, whatever else he is. He has the best of all alibis; the evidence of a man who hates him. I'm not likely to perjure myself for love of Dalmon; and I could swear in any court he did nothing to the old man yesterday. Dalmon and I were together all day, or all that part of the day, and he did nothing in the village except buy cigarettes, and nothing here except smoke them and read in the library. No; I believe he is a criminal, but he did not kill

Vaudrey. I might even say more; because he is a criminal he did not kill Vaudrey."

"Yes," said the other patiently, "and what does that mean?"

"It means," replied the secretary, "that he is a criminal committing another crime: and his crime depends on keeping Vaudrey alive."

"Oh, I see," said Father Brown.

"I know Sybil Rye pretty well, and her character is a great part of this story. It is a very fine character in both senses: that is, it is of a noble quality and only too delicate a texture. She is one of those people who are terribly conscientious, without any of that armour of habit and hard common sense that many conscientious people get. She is almost insanely sensitive and at the same time quite unselfish. Her history is curious: she was left literally penniless like a foundling and Sir Arthur took her into his house and treated her with consideration, which puzzled many; for, without being hard on the old man, it was not much in his line. But, when she was about seventeen, the explanation came to her with a shock; for her guardian asked her to marry him. Now I come to the curious part of the story. Somehow or other, Sybil had heard from somebody (I rather suspect from old Abbott) that Sir Arthur Vaudrey, in his wilder youth, had committed some crime or, at least, done some great wrong to somebody, which had got him into serious trouble. I don't know what it was. But it was a sort of nightmare to the girl at her crude sentimental age, and made him seem like a monster, at least too much so for the close relation of marriage. What she did was incredibly typical of her. With helpless terror and with heroic courage she told him the truth with her own trembling lips. She admitted that her repulsion might be morbid; she confessed it like a secret madness. To her relief and surprise he took it quietly and courteously, and apparently said no more on the subject; and her sense of his generosity was greatly increased by the next stage of the story. There came into her lonely life the influence of an equally lonely man. He was camping-out like a sort of hermit on one of the islands in the river; and I suppose the mystery made him attractive, though I admit he is attractive enough; a gentleman, and quite witty, though very melancholy—which, I suppose, increased the romance. It was this man, Dalmon, of course; and to this day I'm not sure how far she really accepted him; but it got as far as his getting permission to see her guardian. I can fancy her awaiting that interview in an agony of terror and wondering how the old beau would take the appearance of a rival. But here, again, she found she had apparently done him an injustice. He received the younger man with hearty hospitality and seemed to be delighted with the prospects of the young couple. He and Dalmon went shooting and fishing together and were the best of friends, when one day she had another shock. Dalmon let slip in conversation some chance phrase that the old man 'had not changed much in thirty years,' and the truth about the odd intimacy burst upon her. All that introduction and hospitality had been a masquerade; the men had obviously known each other before. That was why the younger man had come down rather covertly to that district. That was why the elder man was lending himself so readily to promote the match. I wonder what you are thinking?"

"I know what you are thinking," said Father Brown, with a smile, "and it seems entirely logical. Here we have Vaudrey, with some ugly story in his past—a mysterious stranger come to haunt him, and getting whatever he wants out of him. In plain words, you think Dalmon is a blackmailer."

"I do," said the other; "and a rotten thing to think, too."

Father Brown reflected for a moment and then said: "I think I should like to go up to the house now and have a talk to Dr. Abbott."

When he came out of the house again an hour or two afterwards, he may have been talking to Dr. Abbott, but he emerged in company with Sybil Rye, a pale girl with reddish hair and a profile delicate and almost tremulous; at the sight other, one could instantly understand all the secretary's story of her shuddering candour. It recalled Godiva and certain tales of virgin martyrs; only the shy can be so shameless for conscience's sake. Smith came forward to meet them, and for a moment they stood talking on the lawn. The day which had been brilliant from daybreak was now glowing and even glaring; but Father Brown carried his black bundle of an umbrella as well as wearing his black umbrella of a hat; and seemed, in a general way, buttoned up to breast the storm. But perhaps it was only an unconscious effect of attitude; and perhaps the storm was not a material storm.

"What I hate about it all," Sybil was saying in a low voice, "is the talk that's beginning already; suspicions against everybody. John and Evan can answer for each other, I suppose; but Dr. Abbott has had an awful scene with the butcher, who thinks he is accused and is throwing accusations about in consequence."

Evan Smith looked very uncomfortable; then blurted out: "Look here, Sybil, I can't say much, but we don't believe there's any need for all that. It's all very beastly, but we don't think there's been — any violence."

'Have you got a theory, then?" said the girl, looking instantly at the priest.

"I have heard a theory," he replied, "which seems to me very convincing."

He stood looking rather dreamily towards the river; and Smith and Sybil began to talk to each other swiftly, in lowered tones. The priest drifted along the river bank, ruminating, and plunged into a plantation of thin trees on an almost overhanging bank. The strong sun beat on the thin veil of little dancing leaves like small green flames, and all the birds were singing as if the tree had a hundred tongues. A minute or two later, Evan Smith heard his own name called cautiously and yet clearly from the green depths of the thicket. He stepped rapidly in that direction and met Father Brown returning. The priest said to him, in a very low voice:

"Don't let the lady come down here. Can't you get rid of her? Ask her to telephone or something; and then come back here again."

Evan Smith turned with a rather desperate appearance of carelessness and approached the girl; but she was not the sort of person whom it is hard to make busy with small jobs for others. In a very short time she had vanished into the house and Smith turned to find that Father Brown had once more vanished into the thicket. Just beyond the clump of trees was a sort of small chasm where the turf had subsided to the level of the sand by the river. Father Brown was standing on the brink of this cleft, looking down; but, either by accident or design, he was holding his hat in his hand, in spite of the strong sun pouring on his head.

"You had better see this yourself," he said, heavily, "as a matter of evidence. But I warn you to be prepared."

"Prepared for what?" asked the other

"Only for the most horrible thing I ever saw in my life," said Father Brown.

Even Smith stepped to the brink of the bank of turf and with difficulty repressed a cry rather like a scream.

Sir Arthur Vaudrey was glaring and grinning up at him; the face was turned up so that he could have put his foot on it; the head was thrown back, with its wig of whitish yellow hair towards him, so that he saw the face upside down. This made it seem all the more like a part of a nightmare; as if a man were walking about with his head stuck on the wrong way. What was he doing? Was it possible that Vaudrey was really creeping about, hiding in the cracks of field and bank, and peering out at them in this unnatural posture? The rest of the figure seemed hunched and almost crooked, as if it had been crippled or deformed but on looking more closely, this seemed only the foreshortening of limbs fallen in a heap. Was he mad? Was he? The more Smith looked at him the stiffer the posture seemed.

"You can't see it from here properly," said Father Brown, "but his throat is cut."

Smith shuddered suddenly. "I can well believe it's the most horrible thing you've seen," he said. "I think it's seeing the face upside down. I've seen that face at breakfast, or dinner, every day for ten years; and it always looked quite pleasant and polite. You turn it upside down and it looks like the face of a fiend."

"The face really is smiling," said Father Brown, soberly; "which is perhaps not the least part of the riddle. Not many men smile while their throats are being cut, even if they do it themselves. That smile, combined with those gooseberry eyes of his that always seemed standing out of his head, is enough, no doubt, to explain the expression. But it's true, things look different upside down. Artists often turn their drawings upside down to test their correctness. Sometimes, when it's difficult to turn the object itself upside down (as in the case of the Matterhorn, let us say), they have been known to stand on their heads, or at least look between their legs."

The priest, who was talking thus flippantly to steady the other man's nerves, concluded by saying, in a more serious tone: "I quite understand how it must have upset you. Unfortunately, it also upset something else."

"What do you mean?"

"It has upset the whole of our very complete theory," replied the other; and he began clambering down the bank on to the little strip of sand by the river.

"Perhaps he did it himself," said Smith abruptly. "After all, that's the most obvious sort of escape, and fits in with our theory very well. He wanted a quiet place and he came here and cut his throat."

"He didn't come here at all," said Father Brown. "At least, not alive, and not by land. He wasn't killed here; there's not enough blood. This sun has dried his hair and clothes pretty well by now; but there are the traces of two trickles of water in the sand. Just about here the tide comes up from the sea and makes an eddy that washed the body into the creek and left it when the tide retired. But the body must first have been washed down the river, presumably from the village, for the river runs just behind the row of little houses and shops. Poor Vaudrey died up in the hamlet, somehow; after all, I don't think he committed suicide; but the trouble is who would, or could, have killed him up in that potty little place?"

He began to draw rough designs with the point of his stumpy umbrella on the strip of sand.

"Let's see; how does the row of shops run? First, the butcher's; well, of course, a butcher would be an ideal performer with a large carving- knife. But you saw Vaudrey come out, and it isn't very probable that he stood in the outer shop while the butcher said: 'Good morning. Allow me to cut your throat! Thank you. And the next article, please?' Sir Arthur doesn't strike me as the sort of man who'd have stood there with a pleasant smile while this happened. He was a very strong and vigorous man, with rather a violent temper. And who else, except the butcher, could have stood up to him? The next shop is kept by an old woman. Then comes the tobacconist, who is certainly a man, but I am told quite a small and timid one. Then there is the dressmaker's, run by two maiden ladies, and then a refreshment shop run by a man who happens to be in hospital and who has left his wife in charge. There are two or three village lads, assistants and errand boys, but they were away on a special job. The refreshment shop ends the street; there is nothing beyond that but the inn, with the policeman between."

He made a punch with the ferrule of his umbrella to represent the policeman, and remained moodily staring up the river. Then he made a slight movement with his hand and, stepping quickly across, stooped over the corpse.

"Ah," he said, straightening himself and letting out a great breath. "The tobacconist! Why in the world didn't I remember that about the tobacconist?"

"What is the matter with you?" demanded Smith in some exasperation; for Father Brown was rolling his eyes and muttering, and he had uttered the word "tobacconist" as if it were a terrible word of doom.

"Did you notice," said the priest, after a pause, "something rather curious about his face?"

"Curious, my God!" said Evan, with a retrospective shudder. "Anyhow, his throat was cut. ..."

"I said his face," said the cleric quietly. "Besides, don't you notice he has hurt his hand and there's a small bandage round it?"

"Oh, that has nothing to do with it," said Evan hastily. "That happened before and was quite an accident. He cut his hand with a broken ink- bottle while we were working together."

"It has something to do with it, for all that," replied Father Brown.

There was a long silence, and the priest walked moodily along the sand, trailing his umbrella and sometimes muttering the word "tobacconist," till the very word chilled his friend with fear. Then he suddenly lifted the umbrella and pointed to a boat-house among the rushes.

"Is that the family boat?" he asked. "I wish you'd just scull me up the river; I want to look at those houses from the back. There's no time to lose. They may find the body; but we must risk that."

Smith was already pulling the little boat upstream towards the hamlet before Father Brown spoke again. Then he said:

"By the way, I found out from old Abbott what was the real story about poor Vaudrey's misdemeanour. It was a rather curious story about an Egyptian official who had insulted him by saying that a good Moslem would avoid swine and Englishmen, but preferred swine; or some such tactful remark. Whatever happened at the time, the quarrel was apparently renewed some years after, when the official visited England; and Vaudrey, in his violent passion, dragged the man to a pig-sty on the farm attached to the country house and threw him in, breaking his arm and leg and leaving him there till next morning. There was rather a row about it, of course, but many people thought Vaudrey had acted in a pardonable passion of patriotism. Anyhow, it seems not quite the thing that would have kept a man silent under deadly blackmail for decades."

"Then you don't think it had anything to do with the story we are considering?" asked the secretary, thoughtfully.

"I think it had a thundering lot to do with the story I am considering now," said Father Brown.

They were now floating past the low wall and the steep strips of back garden running down from the back doors to the river. Father Brown counted them carefully, pointing with his umbrella, and when he came to the third he said again:

"Tobacconist! Is the tobacconist by any chance... .? But I think I'll act on my guess till I know. Only, I'll tell you what it was I thought odd about Sir Arthur's face."

"And what was that?" asked his companion, pausing and resting on his oars for an instant.

"He was a great dandy," said Father Brown, "and the face was only half-shaved. . . . Could you stop here a moment? We could tie up the boat to that post."

A minute or two afterwards they had clambered over the little wall and were mounting the steep cobbled paths of the little garden, with its rectangular beds of vegetables and flowers.

"You see, the tobacconist does grow potatoes," said Father Brown. "Associations with Sir Walter Raleigh, no doubt. Plenty of potatoes and plenty of potato sacks. These little country people have not lost all the habits of peasants; they still run two or three jobs at once. But country tobacconists very often do one odd job extra, that I never thought of till I saw Vaudrey's chin. Nine times out of ten you call the shop the tobacconist's, but it is also the barber's. He'd cut his hand and couldn't shave himself; so he came up here. Does that suggest anything else to you?"

"It suggests a good deal," replied Smith; "but I expect it will suggest a good deal more to you."

"Does it suggest, for instance," observed Father Brown, "the only conditions in which a vigorous and rather violent gentleman might be smiling pleasantly when his throat was cut?"

The next moment they had passed through a dark passage or two at the back of the house, and came into the back room of the shop, dimly lit by filtered light from beyond and a dingy and cracked looking-glass. It seemed, somehow, like the green twilight of a tank; but there was light enough to see the rough apparatus of a barber's shop and the pale and even panic-stricken face of a barber.

Father Brown's eye roamed round the room, which seemed to have been just recently cleaned and tidied, till his gaze found something in a dusty corner just behind the door. It was a hat hanging on a hat-peg. It was a white hat, and one very well known to all that village. And yet, conspicuous as it had always seemed in the street, it seemed only an example of the sort of little thing a certain sort of man often entirely forgets, when he has most carefully washed floors or destroyed stained rags.

"Sir Arthur Vaudrey was shaved here yesterday morning, I think," said Father Brown in a level voice.

To the barber, a small, bald-headed, spectacled man whose name was Wicks, the sudden appearance of these two figures out of his own back premises was like the appearance of two ghosts risen out of a grave under the floor. But it was at once apparent that he had more to frighten him than any fancy of superstition. He shrank, we might almost say that he shrivelled, into a corner of the dark room; and everything about him seemed to dwindle, except his great goblin spectacles.

"Tell me one thing," continued the priest, quietly. "You had a reason for hating the squire?"

The man in the corner babbled something that Smith could not hear; but the priest nodded.

"I know you had," be said. "You hated him; and that's how I know you didn't kill him. Will you tell us what happened, or shall I?"

There was a silence filled with the faint ticking of a clock in the back kitchen; and then Father Brown went on.

"What happened was this. When Mr. Dalmon stepped inside your outer shop, he asked for some cigarettes that were in the window. You stepped outside for a moment, as shopmen often do, to make sure of what he meant; and in that moment of time he perceived in the inner room the razor you had just laid down, and the yellow-white head of Sir Arthur in the barber's chair; probably both glimmering in the light of that little window beyond. It took but an instant for him to pick up the razor and cut the throat and come back to the counter. The victim would not even be alarmed at the razor and the hand. He died smiling at his own thoughts. And what thoughts! Nor, I think, was Dalmon alarmed. He had done it so quickly and quietly that Mr. Smith here could have sworn in court that the two were together all the time. But there was somebody who was alarmed, very legitimately, and that was you. You had quarrelled with your landlord about arrears of rent and so on; you came back into your own shop and found your enemy murdered in your own chair, with your own razor. It was not altogether unnatural that you despaired of clearing yourself, and preferred to clear up the mess; to clean the floor and throw the corpse into the river at night, in a potato sack rather loosely tied. It was rather lucky that there were fixed hours after which your barber's shop was shut; so you had plenty of time. You seem to have remembered everything but the hat. . . . Oh, don't be frightened; I shall forget everything, including the hat."

And he passed placidly through the outer shop into the street beyond, followed by the wondering Smith, and leaving behind the barber stunned and staring.

"You see," said Father Brown to his companion, "it was one of those cases where a motive really is too weak to convict a man and yet strong enough to acquit him. A little nervous fellow like that would be the last man really to kill a big strong man for a tiff about money. But he would be the first man to fear that he would be accused of having done it. ... Ah, there was a thundering difference in the motive of the man who did do it." And he relapsed into reflection, staring and almost glaring at vacancy.

"It is simply awful," groaned Evan Smith. "I was abusing Dalmon as a blackmailer and a blackguard an hour or two ago, and yet it breaks me all up to hear he really did this, after all."

The priest still seemed to be in a sort of trance, like a man staring down into an abyss. At last his lips moved and he murmured, more as if it were a prayer than an oath: "Merciful God, what a horrible revenge!"

His friend questioned him, but he continued as if talking to himself.

"What a horrible tale of hatred! What a vengeance for one mortal worm to take on another! Shall we ever get to the bottom of this bottomless human heart, where such abominable imaginations can abide? God save us all from pride; but I cannot yet make any picture in my mind of hate and vengeance like that."

"Yes," said Smith; "and I can't quite picture why he should kill Vaudrey at all. If Dalmon was a blackmailer, it would seem more natural for Vaudrey to kill him. As you say, the throat-cutting was a horrid business, but — —"

Father Brown started, and blinked like a man awakened from sleep.

"Oh, that!" he corrected hastily. "I wasn't thinking about that. I didn't mean the murder in the barber's shop, when — when I said a horrible tale of vengeance. I was thinking of a much more horrible tale than that; though, of course, that was horrible enough, in its way. But that was much more comprehensible; almost anybody might have done it. In fact, it was very nearly an act of self-defence."

"What?" exclaimed the secretary incredulously. "A man creeps up behind another man and cuts his throat, while he is smiling pleasantly at the ceiling in a barber's chair, and you say it was self-defence!"

"I do not say it was justifiable self-defence," replied the other. "I only say that many a man would have been driven to it, to defend himself against an appalling calamity — which was also an appalling crime. It was that other crime that I was thinking about. To begin with, about that question you asked just now — why should the blackmailer be the murderer? Well, there are a good many conventional confusions and errors on a point like that." He paused, as if collecting his thoughts after his recent trance of horror, and went on in ordinary tones.

"You observe that two men, an older and a younger, go about together and agree on a matrimonial project; but the origin of their intimacy is old and concealed. One is rich and the other poor; and you guess at blackmail. You are quite right, at least to that extent. Where you are quite wrong is in guessing which is which. You assume that the poor man was blackmailing the rich man. As a matter offset, the rich man was blackmailing the poor man."

"But that seems nonsense," objected the secretary.

"It is much worse than nonsense; but it is not at all uncommon," replied the other. "Half modern politics consists of rich men blackmailing people. Your notion that it's nonsense rests on two illusions which are both nonsensical. One is, that rich men never want to be richer; the other is, that a man can only be blackmailed for money. It's the last that is in question here. Sir Arthur Vaudrey was acting not for avarice, but for vengeance. And he planned the most hideous vengeance I ever heard of."

"But why should he plan vengeance on John Dalmon?" inquired Smith.

"It wasn't on John Dalmon that he planned vengeance," replied the priest, gravely.

There was a silence; and he resumed, almost as if changing the subject. "When we found the body, you remember, we saw the face upside down; and you said it looked like the face of a fiend. Has it occurred to you that the murderer also saw the face upside down, coming behind the barber's chair?"

"But that's all morbid extravagance," remonstrated his companion. "I was quite used to the face when it was the right way up."

"Perhaps you have never seen it the right way up," said Father Brown. "I told you that artists turn a picture the wrong way up when they want to see it the right way up. Perhaps, over all those breakfasts and tea- tables, you had got used to the face of a fiend."

"What on earth are you driving at?" demanded Smith, impatiently.

"I speak in parables," replied the other in a rather sombre tone "Of course, Sir Arthur was not actually a fiend; he was a man with a character which he had made out of a temperament that might also have been turned to good. But those goggling, suspicious eyes; that tight, yet quivering mouth, might have told you something if you had not been so used to them. You know, there are physical bodies on which a wound will not heal. Sir Arthur had a mind of that sort. It was as if it lacked a skin; he had a feverish vigilance of vanity; those strained eyes were open with an insomnia of egoism. Sensibility need not be selfishness. Sybil Rye, for instance, has the same thin skin and manages to be a sort of saint. But Vaudrey had turned it all to poisonous pride; a pride that was not even secure and self-satisfied. Every scratch on the surface of his soul festered. And that is the meaning of that old story about throwing the man into the pig-sty. If he'd thrown him then and there, after being called a pig, it might have been a pardonable burst of passion. But there was no pig-sty; and that is just the point. Vaudrey remembered the silly insult for years and years, till he could get the Oriental into the improbable neighbourhood of a pig-sty; and then he took, what he considered the only appropriate and artistic revenge. . . . Oh, my God! He liked his revenges to be appropriate and artistic."

Smith looked at him curiously. "You are not thinking of the pig-sty story," he said.

"No," said Father Brown; "of the other story." He controlled the shudder in his voice, and went on:

"Remembering that story of a fantastic and yet patient plot to make the vengeance fit the crime, consider the other story before us. Had anybody else, to your knowledge, ever insulted Vaudrey, or offered him what he thought a mortal insult? Yes; a woman insulted him."

A sort of vague horror began to dawn in Evan's eyes; he was listening intently.

"A girl, little more than a child, refused to marry him, because he had once been a sort of criminal; had, indeed, been in prison for a short time for the outrage on the Egyptian. And that madman said, in the hell of his heart: 'She shall marry a murderer.'"

They took the road towards the great house and went along by the river for some time in silence, before he resumed: "Vaudrey was in a position to blackmail Dalmon, who had committed a murder long ago; probably he knew of several crimes among the wild comrades of his youth. Probably it was a wild crime with some redeeming features; for the wildest murders are never the worst. And Dalmon looks to me like a man who knows remorse, even for killing Vaudrey. But he was in Vaudrey's power and, between them, they entrapped the girl very cleverly into an engagement; letting the lover try his luck first, for instance, and the other only encouraging magnificently. But Dalmon himself did not know, nobody but the Devil himself did know, what was really in that old man's mind.

"Then, a few days ago, Dalmon made a dreadful discovery. He had obeyed, not altogether unwillingly; he had been a tool; and he suddenly found how the tool was to be broken and thrown away. He came upon certain notes of Vaudrey's in the library which, disguised as they were, told of preparations for giving information to the police. He understood the whole plot and stood stunned as I did when I first understood it. The moment the bride and bridegroom were married, the bridegroom would be arrested and hanged. The fastidious lady, who objected to a husband who had been in prison, should have no husband except a husband on the gallows. That is what Sir Arthur Vaudrey considered an artistic rounding off of the story."

Evan Smith, deadly pale, was silent; and, far away, down the perspective of the road, they saw the large figure and wide hat of Dr. Abbott advancing towards them; even in the outline there was a certain agitation. But they were still shaken with their own private apocalypse.

"As you say, hate is a hateful thing," said Evan at last; "and, do you know, one thing gives me a sort of relief. All my hatred of poor Dalmon is gone out of me—now I know how he was twice a murderer."

It was in silence that they covered the rest of the distance and met the big doctor coming towards them, with his large gloved hands thrown out in a sort of despairing gesture and his grey beard tossing in the wind.

"There is dreadful news," he said. "Arthur's body has been found. He seems to have died in his garden."

"Dear me," said Father Brown, rather mechanically. "How dreadful!"

"And there is more," cried the doctor breathlessly. "John Dalmon went off to see Vernon Vaudrey, the nephew; but Vernon Vaudrey hasn't heard of him and Dalmon seems to have disappeared entirely."

"Dear me," said Father Brown. "How strange!"

VII: THE WORST CRIME IN THE WORLD

FATHER BROWN was wandering through a picture gallery with an expression that suggested that he had not come there to look at the pictures. Indeed, he did not want to look at the pictures, though he liked pictures well enough. Not that there was anything immoral or improper about those highly modern pictorial designs. He would indeed be of an inflammable temperament who was stirred to any of the more pagan passions by the display of interrupted spirals, inverted cones and broken cylinders with which the art of the future inspired or menaced mankind. The truth is that Father Brown was looking for a young friend who had appointed that somewhat incongruous meeting-place, being herself of a more futuristic turn. The young friend was also a young relative; one of the few relatives that he had. Her name was Elizabeth Fane, simplified into Betty, and she was the child of a sister who had married into a race of refined but impoverished squires. As the squire was dead as well as impoverished, Father Brown stood in the relation of a protector as well as a priest, and in some sense a guardian as well is an uncle. At the moment, however, he was blinking about at the groups in the gallery without catching sight of the familiar brown hair and bright face of his niece. Nevertheless, he saw some people he knew and a number of people he did not know, including some that, as a mere matter of taste, he did not much want to know.

Among the people the priest did not know and who yet aroused his interest was a lithe and alert young man, very beautifully dressed and looking rather like a foreigner, because, while his beard was cut in a spade shape like an old Spaniard's, his dark hair was cropped so close as to look like a tight black skull-cap. Among the people the priest did not particularly want to know was a very dominant-looking lady, sensationally clad in scarlet, with a mane of yellow hair too long to be called bobbed, but too loose to be called anything else. She had a powerful and rather heavy face of a pale and rather unwholesome complexion, and when she looked at anybody she cultivated the fascinations of a basilisk. She towed in attendance behind her a short man with a big beard and a very broad face, with long sleepy slits of eyes. The expression of his face was beaming and benevolent, if only partially awake; but his bull neck, when seen from behind, looked a little brutal.

Father Brown gazed at the lady, feeling that the appearance and approach of his niece would be an agreeable contrast. Yet he continued to gaze, for some reason, until he reached the point of feeling that the appearance of anybody would be an agreeable contrast. It was therefore with a certain relief, though with a slight start as of awakening, that he turned at the sound of his name and saw another face that he knew.

It was the sharp but not unfriendly face of a lawyer named Granby, whose patches of grey hair might almost have been the powder from a wig, so incongruous were they with his youthful energy of movement. He was one of those men in the City who run about like schoolboys in and out of their offices. He could not run round the fashionable picture gallery quite in that fashion; but he looked as if he wanted to, and fretted as he glanced to left and right, seeking somebody he knew.

"I didn't know," said Father Brown, smiling, "that you were a patron of the New Art."

"I didn't know that you were," retorted the other. "I came here to catch a man."

"I hope you will have good sport," answered the priest. "I'm doing much the same."

"Said he was passing through to the Continent," snorted the solicitor, "and could I meet him in this cranky place." He ruminated a moment, and said abruptly: "Look here, I know you can keep a secret. Do you know Sir John Musgrave?"

"No," answered the priest; "but I should hardly have thought he was a secret, though they say be does hide himself in a castle. Isn't he the old man they tell all those tales about — how he lives in a tower with a real portcullis and drawbridge, and generally refuses to emerge from the Dark Ages? Is he one of your clients?"

"No," replied Granby shortly: "it's his son, Captain Musgrave, who has come to us. But the old man counts for a good deal in the affair, and I don't know him; that's the point. Look here, this is confidential, as I say, but I can confide in you.' He dropped his voice and drew his friend apart into a side gallery containing representations of various real objects, which was comparatively empty.

"This young Musgrave," he said, "wants to raise a big sum from us on a post obit on his old father in Northumberland. The old man's long past seventy and presumably will obit some time or other; but what about the post, so to speak? What will happen afterwards to his cash and castles and portcullises and all the rest? It's a very fine old estate, and still worth a lot, but strangely enough it isn't entailed. So you see how we stand. The question is, as the man said in Dickens, is the old man friendly?"

"If he's friendly to his son you'll feel all the friendlier," observed Father Brown. "No, I'm afraid I can't help you. I never met Sir John Musgrave, and I understand very few people do meet him nowadays. But it seems obvious you have a right to an answer on that point before you lend the young gentleman your firm's money. Is he the sort that people cut off with a shilling?"

"Well, I'm doubtful," answered the other. "He's very popular and brilliant and a great figure in society; but he's a great deal abroad, and he's been a journalist."

"Well," said Father Brown, "that's not a crime. At least not always."

"Nonsense!" said Granby curtly. "You know what I mean—he's rather a rolling stone, who's been a journalist and a lecturer and an actor, and all sorts of things. I've got to know where I stand. . . . Why, there he is."

And the solicitor, who had been stamping impatiently about the emptier gallery, turned suddenly and darted into the more crowded room at a run. He was running towards the tall and well-dressed young man with the short hair and the foreign-looking beard.

The two walked away together talking, and for some moments afterwards Father Brown followed them with his screwed, short-sighted eyes. His gaze was shifted and recalled, however, by the breathless and even boisterous arrival of his niece, Betty. Rather to the surprise of her uncle, she led him back into the emptier room and planted him on a seat that was like an island in that sea of floor.

"I've got something I must tell you," she said. "It's so silly that nobody else will understand it."

"You overwhelm me," said Father Brown. "Is it about this business your mother started telling me about? Engagements and all that; not what the military historians call a general engagement."

"You know," she said, "that she wants me to be engaged to Captain Musgrave."

"I didn't," said Father Brown with resignation; "but Captain Musgrave seems to be quite a fashionable topic."

"Of course we're very poor," she said, "and it's no good saying it makes no difference."

"Do you want to marry him?" asked Father Brown, looking at her through his half-closed eyes.

She frowned at the floor, and answered in a lower tone:

"I thought I did. At least I think I thought I did. But I've just had rather a shock."

"Then tell us all about it."

"I heard him laugh," she said.

"It is an excellent social accomplishment," he replied.

"You don't understand," said the girl. "It wasn't social at all. That was just the point of it—that it wasn't social."

She paused a moment, and then went on firmly: "I came here quite early, and saw him sitting quite alone in the middle of that gallery with the new pictures, that was quite empty then. He had no idea I or anybody was near; he was sitting quite alone, and he laughed."

"Well, no wonder,' said Father Brown. "I'm not an art critic myself, but as a general view of the pictures taken as a whole — — "

"Oh, you won't understand," she said almost angrily. "It wasn't a bit like that. He wasn't looking at the pictures. He was staring right up at the ceiling; but his eyes seemed to be turned inwards, and he laughed so that my blood ran cold."

The priest had risen and was pacing the room with his hands behind him. "You mustn't be hasty in a case of this sort," he began. "There are two kinds of men—but we can hardly discuss him just now, for here he is."

Captain Musgrave entered the room swiftly and swept it with a smile. Granby, the lawyer, was just behind him, and his legal face bore a new expression of relief and satisfaction.

'I must apologize for everything I said about the Captain," he said to the priest as they drifted together towards the door. "He's a thoroughly sensible fellow and quite sees my point. He asked me himself why I didn't go north amd see his old father; I could hear from the old man's own lips how it stood about the inheritance. Well, he couldn't say fairer than that, could he? But he's so anxious to get the thing settled that he offered to take me up in his own car to Musgrave Moss. That's the name of the estate. I suggested that, if he was so kind, we might go together; and we're starting to-morrow morning."

As they spoke Betty and the Captain came through the doorway together, making in that framework at least a sort of picture that some would be sentimental enough to prefer to cones and cylinders. Whatever their other affinities, they were both very good-looking; and the lawyer was moved to a remark on the fact, when the picture abruptly altered.

Captain James Musgrave looked out into the main gallery, and his laughing and triumphant eyes were riveted on something that seemed to change him from head to foot. Father Brown looked round as under an advancing shadow of premonition; and he saw the lowering, almost livid face of the large woman in scarlet under its leonine yellow hair. She always stood with a slight stoop, like a bull lowering its horns, and the expression of her pale pasty face was so oppressive and hypnotic that they hardly saw the little man with the large beard standing beside her.

Musgrave advanced into the centre of the room towards her, almost like a beautifully dressed wax-work wound up to walk. He said a few words to her that could not be heard. She did not answer; but they turned away together, walking down the long gallery as if in debate, the short, bull -necked man with the beard bringing up the rear like some grotesque goblin page.

"Heaven help us!" muttered Father Brown, frowning after them. "Who in the world is that woman?"

"No pal of mine, I'm happy to say," replied Granby with grim flippancy. "Looks as if a little flirtation with her might end fatally, doesn't it?"

"I don't think he's flirting with her," said Father Brown.

Even as he spoke the group in question turned at the end of the gallery and broke up, and Captain Musgrave came back to them in hasty strides.

"Look here," he cried, speaking naturally enough, though they fancied his colour was changed. "I'm awfully sorry, Mr. Granby, but I find I can't come north with you to-morrow. Of course, you will take the car all the same. Please do; I shan't want it. I—I have to be in London for some days. Take a friend with you if you like."

"My friend, Father Brown — — " began the lawyer.

"If Captain Musgrave is really so kind," said Father Brown gravely. "I may explain that I have some status in Mr. Granby's inquiry, and it would be a great relief to my mind if I could go."

Which was how it came about that a very elegant car, with an equally elegant chauffeur, shot north the next day over the Yorkshire moors, bearing the incongruous burden of a priest who looked rather like a black bundle, and a lawyer who had the habit of running about on his feet instead of racing on somebody else's wheels.

They broke their journey very agreeably in one of the great dales of the West Riding, dining and sleeping at a comfortable inn, and starting early next day, began to run along the Northumbrian coast till they reached a country that was a maze of sand dunes and rank sea meadows, somewhere in the heart of which lay the old Border castle which had remained so unique and yet so secretive a monument of the old Border wars. They found it at last, by following a path running beside a long arm of the sea that ran inland, and turned eventually into a sort of rude canal ending in the moat of the castle. The castle really was a castle, of the square, embattled plan that the Normans built everywhere from Galilee to the Grampians. It did really and truly have a portcullis and a drawbridge, and they were very realistically reminded of the fact by an accident that delayed their entrance.

They waded amid long coarse grass and thistle to the bank of the moat which ran in a ribbon of black with dead leaves and scum upon it, like ebony inlaid with a pattern of gold. Barely a yard or two beyond the black ribbon was the other green bank and the big stone pillars of the gateway. But so little, it would seem, had this lonely fastness been approached from outside that when the impatient Granby hallooed across to the dim figures behind the portcullis, they seemed, to have considerable difficulty even in lowering the great rusty drawbridge. It started on its way, turning over like a great falling tower above them, and then stuck, sticking out in mid-air at a threatening angle.

The impatient Granby, dancing upon the bank, called out to his companion:

"Oh, I can't stand these stick-in-the-mud ways! Why, it'd be less trouble to jump."

And with characteristic impetuosity he did jump, landing with a slight stagger in safety on the inner shore. Father Brown's short legs were not adapted to jumping. But his temper was more adapted than most people's to falling with a splash into very muddy water. By the promptitude of his companion he escaped falling in very far. But as he was being hauled up the green, slimy bank, he stopped with bent head, peering at a particular point upon the grassy slope.

"Are you botanizing?" asked Granby irritably. "We've got no time for you to collect rare plants after your last attempt as a diver among the wonders of the deep. Come on, muddy or no, we've got to present ourselves before the baronet."

When they had penetrated into the castle, they were received courteously enough by an old servant, the only one in sight, and after indicating their business were shown into a long-oak-panelled room with latticed windows of antiquated pattern. Weapons of many different centuries hung in balanced patterns on the dark walls, and a complete suit of fourteenth-century armour stood like a sentinel beside the large fireplace. In another long room beyond could be seen, through the half-open door, the dark colours of the rows of family portraits.

"I feel as if I'd got into a novel instead of a house," said the lawyer. "I'd no idea anybody did really keep up the 'Mysteries of Udolpho' in this fashion."

"Yes; the old gentleman certainly carries out his historical craze consistently," answered the priest; "and these things are not fakes, either. It's not done by somebody who thinks all mediaeval people lived at the same time. Sometimes they make up suits of armour out of different bits; but that suit all covered one man, and covered him very completely. You, see it's the late sort of tilting-armour."

"I think he's a late sort of host, if it comes to chat," grumbled Granby. "He's keeping us waiting the devil of a time."

"You must expect everything to go slowly in a place like this," said Father Brown. "I think it's very decent of him to see us at all: two total strangers come to ask him highly personal questions."

And, indeed, when the master of the house appeared they had no reason to complain of their reception; but rather became conscious of something genuine in the traditions of breeding and behaviour that could retain their native dignity without difficulty in that barbarous solitude, and after those long years of rustication and moping. The baronet did not seem either surprised or embarrassed at the rare visitation; though they suspected that he had not had a stranger in his house for a quarter of a lifetime, he behaved as if he had been bowing out duchesses a moment before. He showed neither shyness nor impatience when they touched on the very private matter of their errand; after a little leisurely reflection he seemed to recognize their curiosity as justified under the circumstances. He was a thin, keen-looking old gentleman, with black eyebrows and a long chin, and though the carefully-curled hair he wore was undoubtedly a wig, he had the wisdom to wear the grey wig of an elderly man.

"As regards the question that immediately concerns you," he said, "the answer is very simple indeed. I do most certainly propose to hand on the whole of my property to my son, as my father handed it on to me; and nothing — I say advisedly, nothing — would induce me to take any other course."

"I am most profoundly grateful for the information," answered the lawyer. "But your kindness encourages me to say that you are putting it very strongly. I would not suggest that it is in the least likely that your son would do anything to make you doubt his fitness for the charge. Still, he might — — "

"Exactly," said Sir John Musgrave dryly, "he might. It is rather an understatement to say that he might. Will you be good enough to step into the next room with me for a moment?"

He led them into the further gallery, of which they had already caught a glimpse, and gravely paused before a row of the blackened and lowering portraits.

"This is Sir Roger Musgrave," he said, pointing to a long-faced person in a black periwig. "He was one of the lowest liars and rascals in the rascally time of William of Orange, a traitor to two kings and something like the murderer of two wives. That is his father, Sir Robert, a perfectly honest old cavalier. That is his son, Sir James, one of the noblest of the Jacobite martyrs and one of the first men to attempt some reparation to the Church and the poor. Does it matter that the House of Musgrave, the power, the honour, the authority, descended from one good man to another good man through the interval of a bad one? Edward I governed

England well. Edward III covered England with glory. And yet the second glory came from the first glory through the infamy and imbecility of Edward II, who fawned upon Gaveston and ran away from Bruce. Believe me, Mr. Granby, the greatness of a great house and history is something more than these accidental individuals who carry it on, even though they do not grace it. From father to son our heritage has come down, and from father to son it shall continue. You may assure yourselves, gentlemen, and you may assure my son, that I shall not leave my money to a home for lost cats. Musgrave shall leave it to Musgrave till the heavens fall."

"Yes," said Father Brown thoughtfully; "I see what you mean."

"And we shall be only too glad," said the solicitor, "to convey such a happy assurance to your son."

"You may convey the assurance," said their host gravely, "He is secure in any event of having the castle, the title, the land and the money. There is only a small and merely private addition to that arrangement. Under no circumstances whatever will I ever speak to him as long as I live."

The lawyer remained in the same respectful attitude, but he was now respectfully staring.

"Why, what on earth has he — — "

"I am a private gentleman," said Musgrave, "as well as the custodian of a great inheritance. And my son did something so horrible that he has ceased to be — I will not say a gentleman — but even a human being. It is the worst crime in the world. Do you remember what Douglas said when Marmion, his guest, offered to shake hands with him?"

"Yes," said Father Brown.

"'My castles are my king's alone, from turret to foundation stone,'" said Musgrave. "'The hand of Douglas is his own.'"

He turned towards the other room and showed his rather dazed visitors back into it.

"I hope you will take some refreshment," he said, in the same equable fashion. "If you have any doubt about your movements, I should be delighted to offer you the hospitality of the castle for the night."

"Thank you, Sir John," said the priest in a dull voice, "but I think we had better go."

"I will have the bridge lowered at once," said their host; and in a few moments the creaking of that huge and absurdly antiquated apparatus filled the castle like the grinding of a mill. Rusty as it was, however, it worked successfully this time, and they found themselves standing once more on the grassy bank beyond the moat.

Granby was suddenly shaken by a shudder.

"What in hell was it that his son did?" he cried.

Father Brown made no answer. But when they had driven off again in their car and pursued their journey to a village not far off, called Graystones, where they alighted at the inn of the Seven Stars, the lawyer learned with a little mild surprise that the priest did not propose to travel much farther; in other words, that he had apparently every intention of remaining in the neighbourhood.

"I cannot bring myself to leave it like this," he said gravely. "I will send back the car, and you, of course, may very naturally want to go with it. Your question is answered; it is simply whether your firm can afford to lend money on young Musgrave's prospects. But my question isn't answered; it is whether he is a fit husband for Betty. I must try to discover whether he's really done something dreadful, or whether it's the delusion of an old lunatic."

"But," objected the lawyer, "if you want to find out about him, why don't you go after him? Why should you hang about in this desolate hole where he hardly ever comes?"

"What would be the use of my going after him?" asked the other. There's no sense in going up to a fashionable young man in Bond Street and saying: 'Excuse me, but have you committed a crime too horrible for a human being?' If he's bad enough to do it, he's certainly bad enough to deny it. And we don't even know what it is. No, there's only one man that knows, and may tell, in some further outburst of dignified eccentricity. I'm going to keep near him for the present."

And in truth Father Brown did keep near the eccentric baronet, and did actually meet him on more than one occasion, with the utmost politeness on both sides. For the baronet, in spite of his years, was very vigorous and a great walker, and could often be seen stumping through the village, and along the country lanes. Only the day after their arrival, Father Brown, coming out of the inn on to the cobbled market-place, saw the dark and distinguished figure stride past in the direction of the post office. He was very quietly dressed in black, but his strong face was even more arresting in the strong sunlight; with his silvery hair, swarthy eyebrows and long chin, he had something of a reminiscence of Henry Irving, or some other famous actor. In spite of his hoary hair, his figure as well as his face suggested strength, and he carried his stick more like a cudgel than a crutch. He saluted the priest, and spoke with the same air of coming fearlessly to the point which had marked his revelations of yesterday.

"If you are still interested in my son," he said, using the term with an icy indifference, "you will not see very much of him. He has just left the country. Between ourselves, I might say fled the country."

"Indeed," said Father Brown with a grave stare.

"Some people I never heard of, called Grunov, have been pestering me, of all people, about his whereabouts," said Sir John; "and I've just come in to send off a wire to tell them that, so far as I know, he's living in the Poste Restante, Riga. Even that has been a nuisance. I came in yesterday to do it, but was five minutes too late for the post office. Are you staying long? I hope you will pay me another visit."

When the priest recounted to the lawyer his little interview with old Musgrave in the village, the lawyer was both puzzled and interested. "Why has the Captain bolted?" he asked. "Who are the other people who want him? Who on earth are the Grunovs?"

"For the first, I don't know," replied Father Brown. "Possibly his mysterious sin has come to light. I should rather guess that the other people are blackmailing him about it. For the third, I think I do know. That horrible fat woman with yellow hair is called Madame Grunov, and that little man passes as her husband."

The next day Father Brown came in rather wearily, and threw down his black bundle of an umbrella with the air of a pilgrim laying down his staff. He had an air of some depression. But it was as it was so often in his criminal investigations. It was not the depression of failure, but the depression of success.

"It's rather a shock," he said in a dull voice; "but I ought to have guessed it. I ought to have guessed it when I first went in and saw the thing standing there."

"'When you saw what?" asked Granby impatiently.

"When I saw there was only one suit of armour," answered Father Brown. There was a silence during which the lawyer only stared at his friend, and then the friend resumed.

"Only the other day I was just going to tell my niece that there are two types of men who can laugh when they are alone. One might almost say the man who does it is either very good or very bad. You see, he is either confiding the joke to God or confiding it to the Devil. But anyhow he has an inner life. Well, there really is a kind of man who confides the joke to the Devil. He does not mind if nobody sees the joke; if nobody can safely be allowed even to know the joke. The joke is enough in itself, if it is sufficiently sinister and malignant."

"But what are you talking about?" demanded Granby. "Whom are you talking about? Which of them, I mean? Who is this person who is having a sinister joke with his Satanic Majesty?"

Father Brown looked across at him with a ghastly smile.

"Ah," he said, "that's the joke."

There was another silence, but this time the silence seemed to be rather full and oppressive than merely empty; it seemed to settle down on them like the twilight that was gradually turning from dusk to dark. Father Brown went on speaking in a level voice, sitting stolidly with his elbows on the table.

"I've been locking up the Musgrave family," he said. "They are vigorous and long-lived stock, and even in the ordinary way I should think you would wait a good time for your money."

"We're quite prepared for that," answered the solicitor; "but anyhow it can't last indefinitely. The old man is nearly eighty, though he still walks about, and the people at the inn here laugh and say they don't believe he will ever die."

Father Brown jumped up with one of his rare but rapid movements, but remained with his hands on the table, leaning forward and looking his friend in the face.

"That's it," he cried in a low but excited voice. "That's the only problem. That's the only real difficulty. How will he die? How on earth is he to die?"

"What on earth do you mean?" asked Granby.

"I mean," came the voice of the priest out of the darkening room, "that I know the crime that James Musgrave committed."

His tones had such a chill in them that Granby could hardly repress a shiver; he murmured a further question.

"It was really the worst crime in the world," said Father Brown. "At least, many communities and civilizations have accounted it so. It was always from the earliest times marked out in tribe and village for tremendous punishment. But anyhow, I know now what young Musgrave really did and why he did it."

"And what did he do?" asked the lawyer.

"He killed his father," answered the priest.

The lawyer in his turn rose from his seat and gazed across the table with wrinkled brows.

"But his father is at the castle," he cried in sharp tones.

"His father is in the moat," said the priest, "and I was a fool not to have known it from the first when something bothered me about that suit of armour. Don't you remember the look of that room? How very carefully it was arranged and decorated? There were two crossed battle-axes hung on one side of the fire-place, two crossed battle-axes on the other. There was a round Scottish shield on one wall, a round Scottish shield on the other. And there was a stand of armour guarding one side of the hearth, and an empty space on the other. Nothing will make me believe that a man who arranged all the rest of that room with that exaggerated symmetry left that one feature of it lopsided. There was almost certainly another man in armour. And what has become of him?"

He paused a moment, and then went on in a more matter-of-fact tone; "When you come to think of it, it's a very good plan for a murder, and meets the permanent problem of the disposal of the body. The body could stand inside that complete tilting-armour for hours, or even days, while servants came and went, until the murderer could simply drag it out in the dead of night and lower it into the moat, without even crossing the bridge. And then what a good chance he ran! As soon as the body was at all decayed in the stagnant water there would sooner or later be nothing but a skeleton in fourteenth-century armour, a thing very likely to be found in the moat of an old Border castle. It was unlikely that anybody would look for anything there, but if they did, that would soon be all they would find. And I got some confirmation of that. That was when you said I was looking for a rare plant; it was a plant in a good many senses, if you'll excuse the jest. I saw the marks of two feet sunk so deep into the solid bank I was sure that the man was either very heavy or was carrying something very heavy. Also, by the way, there's another moral from that little incident when I made my celebrated graceful and cat-like leap."

"My brain is rather reeling," said Granby, "but I begin to have some notion of what all this nightmare is about. What about you and your cat - like leap?"

"At the post office to-day," said Father Brown, "I casually confirmed the statement the baronet made to me yesterday, that he had been there just after closing-time on the day previous—that is, not only on the very day we arrived, but at the very time we arrived. Don't you see what that means? It means that he was actually out when we called, and came back while we were waiting; and that was why we had to wait so long. And when I saw that, I suddenly saw a picture that told the whole story.'

"Well," asked the other impatiently, "and what about it?"

"An old man of eighty can walk," said Father Brown. "An old man can even walk a good deal, pottering about in country lanes. But an old man can't jump. He would be an even less graceful jumper than I was. Yet, if the baronet came back while we were waiting, he must have come in as we came in—by jumping the moat—for the bridge wasn't lowered till later. I rather guess he had hampered it himself to delay inconvenient visitors, to judge by the rapidity with which it was repaired. But that doesn't matter. When I saw that fancy picture of the black figure with the grey hair taking a flying leap across the moat I knew instantly that it was a young man dressed up as an old man. And there you have the whole story."

"You mean," said Granby slowly, "that this pleasing youth killed his father, hid the corpse first in the armour and then in the moat, disguised himself and so on?"

"They happened to be almost exactly alike," said the priest. "You could sec from the family portraits how strong the likeness ran. And then you talk of his disguising himself. But in a sense everybody's dress is a disguise. The old man disguised himself in a wig, and the young man in a foreign beard. When he shaved and put the wig on his cropped head he was exactly like his father, with a little make-up. Of course, you understand now why he was so very polite about getting you to come up next day here by car. It was because he himself was coming up that night by train. He got in front of you, committed his crime, assumed his disguise, and was ready for the legal negotiations."

"Ah," said Granby thoughtfully, "the legal negotiations! You mean, of course, that the real old baronet would have negotiated very differently.

"He would have told you plainly that the Captain would never get a penny," said Father Brown. "The plot, queer as it sounds, was really the only way of preventing his telling you so. But I want you to appreciate the cunning of what the fellow did tell you. His plan answered several purposes at once. He was being blackmailed by these Russians for some villainy; I suspect for treason during the war. He escaped from them at a stroke, and probably sent them chasing off to Riga after him. But the most beautiful refinement of all was that theory he enunciated about recognizing his son as an heir, but not as a human being. Don't you see that while it secured the post obit, it also provided some sort of answer to what would soon be the greatest difficulty of all?"

"I see several difficulties," said Granby; "which one do you mean?"

"I mean that if the son was not even disinherited, it would look rather odd that the father and son never met. The theory of a private repudiation answered that. So there only remained one difficulty, as I say, which is probably perplexing the gentleman now. How on earth is the old man to die?"

"I know how he ought to die," said Granby.

Father Brown seemed to be a little bemused, and went on in a more abstracted fashion.

"And yet there is something more in it than that," he said. "There was something about that theory that he liked in a way that is more — well, more theoretical. It gave him an insane intellectual pleasure to tell you in one character that he had committed a crime in another character — when he really had. That is what I mean by the infernal irony; by the joke shared with the Devil. Shall I tell you something that sounds like what they call a paradox? Sometimes it is a joy in the very heart of hell to tell the truth. And above all, to tell it so that everybody misunderstands it. That is why he liked that antic of pretending to be somebody else, and then painting himself as black — as he was. And that was why my niece heard him laughing to himself all alone in the picture gallery."

Granby gave a slight start, like a person brought back to common things with a bump.

"Your niece," he cried. "Didn't her mother want her to marry Musgrave? A question of wealth and position, I suppose."

"Yes," said Father Brown dryly; "her mother was all in favour of a prudent marriage."

VIII: THE RED MOON OF MERU

EVERYONE agreed that the bazaar at Mallowood Abbey (by kind permission of Lady Mounteagle) was a great success; there were roundabouts and swings and side-shows, which the people greatly enjoyed; I would also mention the Charity, which was the excellent object of the proceedings, if any of them could tell me what it was. However, it is only with a few of them that we are here concerned; and especially with three of them, a lady and two gentlemen, who passed between two of the principal tents or pavilions, their voices high in argument. On their right was the tent of the Master of the Mountain, that world-famous fortune-teller by crystals and chiromancy; a rich purple tent, all over which were traced, in black and gold, the sprawling outlines of Asiatic gods waving any number of arms like octopods. Perhaps they symbolized the readiness of divine help to be had within; perhaps they merely implied that the ideal being of a pious palmist would have as many hands as possible. On the other side stood the plainer tent of Phroso the Phrenologist; more austerely decorated with diagrams of the heads of Socrates and Shakespeare, which were apparently of a lumpy sort. But these were presented merely in black and white, with numbers and notes, as became the rigid dignity of a purely rationalistic science. The purple tent had an opening like a black cavern, and all was fittingly silent within. But Phroso the Phrenologist, a lean, shabby, sunburnt person, with an almost improbably fierce black moustache and whiskers, was standing outside his own temple, and talking, at the top of his voice, to nobody in particular, explaining that the head of any passer-by would doubtless prove, on examination, to be every bit as knobbly as Shakespeare's. Indeed, the moment the lady appeared between the tents, the vigilant Phroso leapt on her and offered, with a pantomime of old-world courtesy, to feel her bumps.

She refused with civility that was rather like rudeness; but she must be excused, because she was in the middle of an argument. She also had to be excused, or at any rate was excused, because she was Lady Mounteagle. She was not a nonentity, however, in any sense; she was at once handsome and haggard, with a hungry look in her deep, dark eyes and something eager and almost fierce about her smile. Her dress was bizarre for the period; for it was before the Great War had left us in our present mood of gravity and recollection. Indeed, the dress was rather like the purple tent; being of a semi-oriental sort, covered with exotic and esoteric emblems. But everyone knew that the Mounteagles were mad; which was the popular way of saying that she and her husband were interested in the creeds and culture of the East.

The eccentricity of the lady was a great contrast to the conventionality of the two gentlemen, who were braced and buttoned up in all the stiffer fashion of that far-off day, from the tips of their gloves to their bright top hats. Yet even here there was a difference; for James Hardcastle managed at once to look correct and distinguished, while Tommy Hunter only looked correct and commonplace. Hardcastle was a promising politician; who seemed in society to be interested in everything except politics. It may be answered gloomily that every politician is emphatically a promising politician. But to do him justice, he had often exhibited himself as a performing politician. No purple tent in the bazaar, however, had been provided for him to perform in.

"For my part," he said, screwing in the monocle that was the only gleam in his hard, legal face, "I think we must exhaust the possibilities of mesmerism before we talk about magic. Remarkable psychological powers undoubtedly exist, even in apparently backward peoples. Marvellous things have been done by fakirs."

"Did you say done by fakers?" asked the other young man, with doubtful innocence.

"Tommy, you are simply silly," said the lady. "Why will you keep barging in on things you don't understand? You're like a schoolboy screaming out that he knows how a conjuring trick is done. It's all so Early Victorian — that schoolboy scepticism. As for mesmerism, I doubt whether you can stretch it to — — "

At this point Lady Mounteagle seemed to catch sight of somebody she wanted; a black stumpy figure standing at a booth where children were throwing hoops at hideous table ornaments. She darted across and cried:

"Father Brown, I've been looking for you. I want to ask you something, Do you believe in fortune-telling?"

The person addressed looked rather helplessly at the little hoop in his hand and said at last:

"I wonder in which sense you're using the word 'believe.' Of course, if it's all a fraud — — "

"Oh, but the Master of the Mountain isn't a bit of a fraud," she cried. "He isn't a common conjurer or a fortune-teller at all. It's really a great honour for him to condescend to tell fortunes at my parties; he's a great religious leader in his own country; a Prophet and a Seer. And even his fortune-telling isn't vulgar stuff about coming into a fortune. He tells you great spiritual truths about yourself, about your ideals."

"Quite so," said Father Brown. "That's what I object to. I was just going to say that if it's all a fraud, I don't mind it so much. It can't be much more of a fraud than most things at fancy bazaars; and there, in a way, it's a sort of practical joke. But if it's a religion and reveals spiritual truths — then it's all as false as hell and I wouldn't touch it with a bargepole."

"That is something of a paradox," said Hardcastle, with a smile.

"I wonder what a paradox is," remarked the priest in a ruminant manner. "It seems to me obvious enough. I suppose it wouldn't do very much harm if somebody dressed up as a German spy and pretended to have told all sorts of lies to the Germans. But if a man is trading in the truth with the Germans — well! So I think if a fortune-teller is trading in truth like that — — "

"You really think," began Hardcastle grimly.

"Yes," said the other; "I think he is trading with the enemy."

Tommy Hunter broke into a chuckle. "Well," he said, "if Father Brown thinks they're good so long as they're frauds, I should think he'd consider this copper-coloured prophet a sort of saint."

"My cousin Tom is incorrigible," said Lady Mounteagle. "He's always going about showing up adepts, as he calls it. He only came down here in a hurry when he heard the Master was to be here, I believe. He'd have tried to show up Buddha or Moses."

"Thought you wanted looking after a bit," said the young man, with a grin on his round face. "So I toddled down. Don't like this brown monkey crawling about."

"There you go again!" said Lady Mounteagle. "Years ago, when I was in India, I suppose we all had that sort of prejudice against brown people. But now I know something about their wonderful spiritual powers, I'm glad to say I know better."

"Our prejudices seem to cut opposite ways," said Father Brown. "You excuse his being brown because he is brahminical; and I excuse his being brahminical because he is brown. Frankly, I don't care for spiritual powers much myself. I've got much more sympathy with spiritual weaknesses. But I can't see why anybody should dislike him merely because he is the same beautiful colour as copper, or coffee, or nut- brown ale, or those jolly peat-streams in the North. But then," he added, looking across at the lady and screwing up his eyes, "I suppose I'm prejudiced in favour of anything that's called brown."

"There now!" cried Lady Mounteagle with a sort of triumph. "I knew you were only talking nonsense!"

"Well," grumbled the aggrieved youth with the round face. "When anybody talks sense you call it schoolboy scepticism. When's the crystal-gazing going to begin?"

"Any time you like, I believe," replied the lady. "It isn't crystal- gazing, as a matter of fact, but palmistry; I suppose you would say it was all the same sort of nonsense."

"I think there is a via media between sense and nonsense," said Hardcastle, smiling. "There are explanations that are natural and not at all nonsensical; and yet the results are very amazing. Are you coming in to be operated on? I confess I am full of curiosity."

"Oh, I've no patience with such nonsense," spluttered the sceptic, whose round face had become rather a red face with the heat of his contempt and incredulity. "I'll let you waste your time on your mahogany mountebank; I'd rather go and throw at coco-nuts."

The Phrenologist, still hovering near, darted at the opening.

"Heads, my dear sir," he said, "human skulls are of a contour far more subtle than that of coco-nuts. No coco-nut can compare with your own most — — "

Hardcastle had already dived into the dark entry of the purple tent; and they heard a low murmur of voices within. As Tom Hunter turned on the Phrenologist with an impatient answer, in which he showed a regrettable indifference to the line between natural and preternatural sciences, the lady was just about to continue her little argument with the little priest, when she stopped in some surprise. James Hardcastle had come out of the tent again, and in his grim face and glaring monocle, surprise was even

117

more vividly depicted. "He's not there," remarked the politician abruptly. "'He's gone. Some aged nigger, who seems to constitute his suite, jabbered something I to me to the effect that the Master had gone forth rather than sell sacred secrets for gold."

Lady Mounteagle turned radiantly to the rest. "There now," she cried. "I told you he was a cut above anything you fancied! He hates being here in a crowd; he's gone back to his solitude."

"I am sorry," said Father Brown gravely. "I may have done him an injustice. Do you know where he has gone?"

"I think so," said his hostess equally gravely. "When he wants to be alone, he always goes to the cloisters, just at the end of the left wing, beyond my husband's study and private museum, you know. Perhaps you know this house was once an abbey."

"I have heard something about it," answered the priest, with a faint smile.

"We'll go there, if you like," said the lady, briskly. "You really ought to see my husband's collection; or the Red Moon at any rate. Haven't you ever heard of the Red Moon of Meru? Yes, it's a ruby."

"I should be delighted to see the collection," said Hardcastle quietly, "'including the Master of the Mountain, if that prophet is one exhibit in the museum." And they all turned towards the path leading to the house.

"All the same," muttered the sceptical Thomas, as he brought up the rear, "I should very much like to know what the brown beast did come here for, if he didn't come to tell fortunes."

As he disappeared, the indomitable Phroso made one more dart after him, almost snatching at his coat-tails. "The bump — —" he began.

"No bump," said the youth, "only a hump. Hump I always have when I come down to see Mounteagle." And he took to his heels to escape the embrace of the man of science.

On their way to the cloisters the visitors had to pass through the long room that was devoted by Lord Mounteagle to his remarkable private museum of Asiatic charms and mascots. Through one open door, in the length of the wall opposite, they could see the Gothic arches and the glimmer of daylight between them, marking the square open space, round the roofed border of which the monks had walked in older days. But they had to pass something that seemed at first sight rather more extraordinary than the ghost of a monk.

It was an elderly gentleman, robed from head to foot in white, with a pale green turban, but a very pink and white English complexion and the smooth white moustaches of some amiable Anglo-Indian colonel. This was Lord Mounteagle, who had taken his Oriental pleasures more sadly, or at least more seriously than his wife. He could talk of nothing whatever, except Oriental religion and philosophy; and had thought it necessary even to dress in the manner of an Oriental hermit. While he was delighted to show his treasures, he seemed to treasure them much more for the truths supposed to be symbolized in them than for their value in collections, let alone cash. Even when he brought out the great ruby, perhaps the only thing of great value in the museum, in a merely monetary sense, he seemed to be much more interested in its name than in its size, let alone its price.

The others were all staring at what seemed a stupendously large red stone, burning like a bonfire seen through a rain of blood. But Lord Mounteagle rolled it loosely in his palm without looking at it; and staring at the ceiling, told them a long tale about the legendary character of Mount Meru, and how, in the Gnostic mythology, it had been the place of the wrestling of nameless primeval powers.

Towards the end of the lecture on the Demiurge of the Gnostics (not forgetting its connexion with the parallel concept of Manichaeus), even the tactful Mr. Hardcastle thought it time to create a diversion. He asked to be allowed to look at the stone; and as evening was closing in, and the long room with its single door was steadily darkening, he stepped out in the cloister beyond, to examine the jewel by a better light. It was then that they first became conscious, slowly and almost creepily conscious, of the living presence of the Master of the Mountain.

The cloister was on the usual plan, as regards its original structure; but the line of Gothic pillars and pointed arches that formed the inner square was linked together all along by a low wall, about waist high, turning the Gothic doors into Gothic windows and giving each a sort of flat window-sill of stone. This alteration was probably of ancient date; but there were other alterations of a quainter sort, which witnessed to the rather unusual individual ideas of Lord and Lady Mounteagle. Between the pillars hung thin curtains, or rather veils, made of beads or light canes, in a continental or southern manner; and on these again could be traced the lines and colours of Asiatic dragons or idols, that contrasted with the grey Gothic framework in which they were suspended. But this, while it further troubled the dying light of the place, was the least of the incongruities of which the company, with very varying feelings, became aware.

In the open space surrounded by the cloisters, there ran, like a circle in a square, a circular path paved with pale stones and edged with some sort of green enamel like an imitation lawn. Inside that, in the very centre, rose the basin of a dark-green fountain, or raised pond, in which water-lilies floated and goldfish flashed to and fro; and high above these, its outline dark against the dying light, was a great green image. Its back was turned to them and its face so completely invisible in the hunched posture that the statue might almost have been headless. But in that mere dark outline, in the dim twilight, some of them could see instantly that it was the shape of no Christian thing.

A few yards away, on the circular path, and looking towards the great green god, stood the man called the Master of the Mountain. His pointed and finely-finished features seemed moulded by some skilful craftsman as a mask of copper. In contrast with this, his dark-grey beard looked almost blue like indigo; it began in a narrow tuft on his chin, and then spread outwards like a great fan or the tail of a bird. He was robed in peacock green and wore on his bald head a high cap of uncommon outline: a head-dress none of them had ever seen before; but it looked rather Egyptian than Indian. The man was standing with staring eyes; wide open, fish-shaped eyes, so motionless that they looked like the eyes painted on a mummy-case. But though the figure of the Master of the Mountain was singular enough, some of the company, including Father Brown, did not look at him; they still looked at the dark-green idol at which he himself was looking.

"This seems a queer thing," said Hardcastle, frowning a little, "to set up in the middle of an old abbey cloister."

"Now, don't tell me you're going to be silly," said Lady Mounteagle. "That's just what we meant; to link up the great religions of East and West; Buddha and Christ. Surely you must understand that all religions are really the same."

"If they are," said Father Brown mildly, "it seems rather unnecessary to go into the middle of Asia to get one."

"Lady Mounteagle means that they are different aspects or facets, as there are of this stone," began Hardcastle; and becoming interested in the new topic, laid the great ruby down on the stone sill or ledge under the Gothic arch. "But it does not follow that we can mix the aspects in one artistic style. You may mix Christianity and Islam, but you can't mix Gothic and Saracenic, let alone real Indian."

As he spoke, the Master of the Mountain seemed to come to life like a cataleptic, and moved gravely round another quarter segment of the circle, and took up his position outside their own row of arches, standing with his back to them and looking now towards the idol's back. It was obvious that he was moving by stages round the whole circle, like a hand round a clock; but pausing for prayer or contemplation.

"What is his religion?" asked Hardcastle, with a faint touch of impatience.

"He says," replied Lord Mounteagle, reverently, "that it is older than Brahminism and purer than Buddhism."

"Oh," said Hardcastle, and continued to stare through his single eyeglass, standing with both his hands in his pockets.

"They say," observed the nobleman in his gentle but didactic voice, "that the deity called the God of Gods is carved in a colossal form in the cavern of Mount Meru — —"

Even his lordship's lecturing serenity was broken abruptly by the voice that came over his shoulder. It came out of the darkness of the museum they had just left, when they stepped out into the cloister. At the sound of it the two younger men looked first incredulous, then furious, and then almost collapsed into laughter.

"I hope I do not intrude," said the urbane and seductive voice of Professor Phroso, that unconquerable wrestler of the truth, "but it occurred to me that some of you might spare a little time for that much despised science of Bumps, which — —"

"Look here," cried the impetuous Tommy Hunter, "I haven't got any bumps; but you'll jolly well have some soon, you — —"

Hardcastle mildly restrained him as he plunged back through the door; and for the moment all the group had turned again and were looking back into the inner room.

It was at that moment that the thing happened. It was the impetuous Tommy, once more, who was the first to move, and this time to better effect. Before anyone else had seen anything, when Hardcastle had barely remembered with a jump that he had left the gem on the stone sill, Tommy was across the cloister with the leap of a cat and, leaning with his head and shoulders out of the aperture between two columns, had cried out in a voice that rang down all the arches: "I've got him!"

In that instant of time, just after they turned, and just before they heard his triumphant cry, they had all seen it happen. Round the corner of one of the two columns, there had darted in and out again a brown or rather bronze-coloured hand, the colour of dead gold; such as they had seen elsewhere. The hand had struck as straight as a striking snake; as instantaneous as the flick of the long tongue of an ant-eater. But it had licked up the jewel. The stone slab of the window-sill shone bare in the pale and fading light.

"I've got him," gasped Tommy Hunter; "but he's wriggling pretty hard. You fellows run round him in front—he can't have got rid of it, anyhow."

The others obeyed, some racing down the corridor and some leaping over the low wall, with the result that a little crowd, consisting of Hardcastle, Lord Mounteagle, Father Brown, and even the undetachable Mr. Phroso of the bumps, had soon surrounded the captive Master of the Mountain, whom Hunter was hanging on to desperately by the collar with one hand, and shaking every now and then in a manner highly insensible to the dignity of Prophets as a class.

"Now we've got him, anyhow," said Hunter, letting go with a sigh. "We've only got to search him. The thing must be here."

Three-quarters of an hour later. Hunter and Hardcastle, their top-hats, ties, gloves, slips and spats somewhat the worse for their recent activities, came face to face in the cloister and gazed at each other.

"Well," asked Hardcastle with restraint, "have you any views on the mystery?"

"Hang it all," replied Hunter; "you can't call it a mystery. Why, we all saw him take it ourselves."

"Yes," replied the other, "but we didn't all see him lose it ourselves. And the mystery is, where has he lost it so that we can't find it?"

"It must be somewhere," said Hunter. "Have you searched the fountain and all round that rotten old god there?"

"I haven't dissected the little fishes," said Hardcastle, lifting his eyeglass and surveying the other. "Are you thinking of the ring of Polycrates?"

Apparently the survey, through the eye-glass, of the round face before him, convinced him that it covered no such meditation on Greek legend.

"It's not on him, I admit," repeated Hunter, suddenly, "unless he's swallowed it."

"Are we to dissect the Prophet, too?" asked the other smiling. "But here comes our host."

"This is a most distressing matter," said Lord Mounteagle, twisting his white moustache with a nervous and even tremulous hand. "Horrible thing to have a theft in one's house, let alone connecting it with a man like the Master. But, I confess, I can't quite make head or tail of the way in which he is talking about it. I wish you'd come inside and see what you think."

They went in together, Hunter falling behind and dropping into conversation with Father Brown, who was kicking his heels round the cloister.

"You must be very strong," said the priest pleasantly. "You held him with one hand; and he seemed pretty vigorous, even when we had eight hands to hold him, like one of those Indian gods."

They took a turn or two round the cloister, talking; and then they also went into the inner room, where the Master of the Mountain was seated on a bench, in the capacity of a captive, but with more of the air of a king.

It was true, as Lord Mounteagle said, that his air and tone were not very easy to understand. He spoke with a serene, and yet secretive sense of power. He seemed rather amused at their suggestions about trivial hiding-places for the gem; and certainly he showed no resentment whatever. He seemed to be laughing, in a still unfathomable fashion at their efforts to trace what they had all seen him take.

"You are learning a little," he said, with insolent benevolence, "of the laws of time and space; about which your latest science is a thousand years behind our oldest religion. You do not even know what is really meant by

123

hiding a thing. Nay, my poor little friends, you do not even know what is meant by seeing a thing; or perhaps you would see this as plainly as I do."

"Do you mean it is here?" demanded Hardcastle harshly.

"Here is a word of many meanings, also," replied the mystic. "But I did not say it was here. I only said I could see it."

There was an irritated silence, and he went on sleepily.

"If you were to be utterly, unfathomably, silent, do you think you might hear a cry from the other end of the world? The cry of a worshipper alone in those mountains, where the original image sits, itself like a mountain. Some say that even Jews and Moslems might worship that image; because it was never made by man. Hark! Do you hear the cry with which he lifts his head and sees in that socket of stone that has been hollow for ages, the one red and angry moon that is the eye of the mountain?"

"Do you really mean," cried Lord Mounteagle, a little shaken, "that you could make it pass from here to Mount Meru? I used to believe you had great spiritual powers, but — — "

"Perhaps," said the Master, "I have more than you will ever believe."

Hardcastle rose impatiently and began to pace the room with his hands in his pockets.

"I never believed so much as you did; but I admit that powers of a certain type may . . . Good God!"

His high, hard voice had been cut off in mid-air, and he stopped staring; the eye-glass fell out of his eye. They all turned their faces in the same direction; and on every face there seemed to be the same suspended animation.

The Red Moon of Meru lay on the stone window-sill, exactly as they had last seen it. It might have been a red spark blown there from a bonfire, or a red rose-petal tossed from a broken rose; but it had fallen in precisely the same spot where Hardcastle had thoughtlessly laid it down.

This time Hardcastle did not attempt to pick it up again; but his demeanour was somewhat notable. He turned slowly and began to stride about the room again; but there was in his movements something masterful, where before it had been only restless. Finally, he brought himself to a standstill in front of the seated Master, and bowed with a somewhat sardonic smile.

"Master," he said, "we all owe you an apology and, what is more important, you have taught us all a lesson. Believe me, it will serve as a lesson as well as a joke. I shall always remember the very remarkable powers you really possess, and how harmlessly you use them. Lady Mounteagle," he went on, turning towards her, "you will forgive me for having addressed the Master first; but it was to you I had the honour of offering this explanation some time ago. I may say that I explained it before it had happened. I told you that most of these things could be interpreted by some kind of hypnotism. Many believe that this is the explanation of all those Indian stories about the mango plant and the boy who climbs a rope thrown into the air. It does not really happen; but the spectators are mesmerized into imagining that it happened. So we were all mesmerized into imagining this theft had happened. That brown hand coming in at the window, and whisking away the gem, was a momentary delusion; a hand in a dream. Only, having seen the stone vanish, we never looked for it where it was before. We plunged into the pond and turned every leaf of the water lilies; we were almost giving emetics to the goldfish. But the ruby has been here all the time."

And he glanced across at the opalescent eyes and smiling bearded mouth of the Master, and saw that the smile was just a shade broader. There was something in it that made the others jump to their feet with an air of sudden relaxation and general, gasping relief.

"This is a very fortunate escape for us all," said Lord Mounteagle, smiling rather nervously. "There cannot be the least doubt it is as you say. It has been a most painful episode and I really don't know what apologies — —"

"I have no complaints," said the Master or the Mountain, still smiling. "You have never touched me at all."

While the rest went off rejoicing, with Hardcastle for the hero of the hour, the little Phrenologist with the whiskers sauntered back towards his preposterous tent. Looking over his shoulder he was surprised to find Father Brown following him.

"Can I feel your bumps?" asked the expert, in his mildly sarcastic tone.

"I don't think you want to feel any more, do you?" said the priest good -humouredly. "You're a detective, aren't you?"

"Yep," replied the other. "Lady Mounteagle asked me to keep an eye on the Master, being no fool, for all her mysticism; and when he left his tent, I could only follow by behaving like a nuisance and a monomaniac. If anybody had come into my tent, I'd have had to look up Bumps in an encyclopaedia."

"Bumps, What Ho She; see Folk-Lore," observed Father Brown, dreamily. "Well, you were quite in the part in pestering people—at a bazaar."

"Rum case, wasn't it?" remarked the fallacious Phrenologist. "Queer to think the thing was there all the time."

"Very queer," said the priest.

Something in his voice made the other man stop and stare.

"Look here!" he cried; "what's the matter with you? What are you looking like that for! Don't you believe that it was there all the time?"

Father Brown blinked rather as if he had received a buffet; then he said slowly and with hesitation: "No, the fact is ... I can't—I can't quite bring myself to believe it."

"You're not the sort of chap," said the other shrewdly, "who'd say that without reason. Why don't you think the ruby had been there all the time?"

"Only because I put it back myself," said Father Brown.

The other man stood rooted to the spot, like one whose hair was standing on end. He opened his mouth without speech.

"Or rather," went on the priest, "I persuaded the thief to let me put it back. I told him what I'd guessed and showed him there was still time for repentance. I don't mind telling you in professional confidence; besides, I don't think the Mounteagles would prosecute, now they've got the thing back, especially considering who stole it."

"Do you mean the Master?" asked the late Phroso.

"No," said Father Brown, "the Master didn't steal it."

"But I don't understand," objected the other. "Nobody was outside the window except the Master; and a hand certainly came from outside."

"The hand came from outside, but the thief came from the inside," said Father Brown.

"We seem to be back among the mystics again. Look here, I'm a practical man; I only wanted to know if it is all right with the ruby — —"

"I knew it was all wrong," said Father Brown, "before I even knew there was a ruby."

After a pause he went on thoughtfully. "Right away back in that argument of theirs, by the tents, I knew things were going wrong. People will tell you that theories don't matter and that logic and philosophy aren't practical. Don't you believe them? Reason is from God, and when things are unreasonable there is something the matter. Now, that quite abstract argument ended with something funny. Consider what the theories were. Hardcastle was a trifle superior and said that all things were perfectly possible; but they were mostly done merely by mesmerism, or clairvoyance; scientific names for philosophical puzzles, in the usual style. But Hunter thought it all sheer fraud and wanted to show it up. By Lady Mounteagle's testimony, he not only went about showing up fortune-tellers and such like, but he had actually come down specially to confront this one. He didn't often come; he didn't get on with Mounteagle, from whom, being a spendthrift, he always tried to borrow; but when he heard the Master was coming, he came hurrying down. Very well. In spite of that, it was Hardcastle who went to consult the wizard and Hunter who refused. He said he'd waste no time on such nonsense; having apparently wasted a lot of his life on proving it to be nonsense. That seems inconsistent. He thought in this case it was crystal- gazing; but he found it was palmistry."

"Do you mean he made that an excuse?" asked his companion, puzzled.

"I thought so at first," replied the priest; "but I know now it was not an excuse, but a reason. He really was put off by finding it was a palmist, because — — "

"Well," demanded the other impatiently.

"Because he didn't want to take his glove off," said Father Brown.

"Take his glove off?" repeated the inquirer.

"If he had," said Father Brown mildly, "we should all have seen that his hand was painted pale brown already. ... Oh, yes, he did come down specially because the Master was here. He came down very fully prepared."

"You mean," cried Phroso, "that it was Hunter's hand, painted brown, that came in at the window? Why, he was with us all the time!"

127

"Go and try it on the spot and you'll find it's quite possible," said the priest. "Hunter leapt forward and leaned out of the window; in a flash he could tear off his glove, tuck up his sleeve, and thrust his hand back round the other side of the pillar, while he gripped the Indian with the other hand and halloed out that he'd caught the thief. I remarked at the time that he held the thief with one hand, where any sane man would have used two. But the other hand was slipping the jewel into his trouser pocket."

There was a long pause and then the ex-Phrenologist said slowly. "Well, that's a staggerer. But the thing stumps me still. For one thing, it doesn't explain the queer behaviour of the old magician himself. If he was entirely innocent, why the devil didn't he say so? Why wasn't he indignant at being accused and searched? Why did he only sit smiling and hinting in a sly way what wild and wonderful things he could do?"

"Ah!" cried Father Brown, with a sharp note in his voice: "there you come up against it! Against everything these people don't and won't understand. All religions are the same, says Lady Mounteagle. Are they, by George! I tell you some of them are so different that the best man of one creed will be callous, where the worst man of another will be sensitive. I told you I didn't like spiritual power, because the accent is on the word; power. I don't say the Master would steal a ruby, very likely he wouldn't; very likely he wouldn't think it worth stealing. It wouldn't be specially his temptation to take jewels; but it would be his temptation to take credit for miracles that didn't belong to him any more than the jewels. It was to that sort of temptation, to that sort of stealing that he yielded today. He liked us to think that he had marvellous mental powers that could make a material object fly through space; and even when he hadn't done it, he allowed us to think he had. The point about private property wouldn't occur primarily to him at all. The question wouldn't present itself in the form: 'Shall I steal this pebble?' but only in the form: 'Could I make a pebble vanish and re- appear on a distant mountain?' The question of whose pebble would strike him as irrelevant. That is what I mean by religious being different. He is very proud of having what he calls spiritual powers. But what he calls spiritual doesn't mean what we call moral. It means rather mental; the power of the mind over matter; the magician controlling the elements. Now we are not like that, even when we are no better; even when we are worse. We, whose fathers at least were Christians, who have

128

grown up under those mediaeval arches even if we bedizen them with all the demons in Asia—we have the very opposite ambition and the very opposite shame. We should all be anxious that nobody should think we had done it. He was actually anxious that everybody should think he had—even when he hadn't. He actually stole the credit of stealing. While we were all casting the crime from us like a snake, he was actually luring it to him like a snake-charmer. But snakes are not pets in this country! Here the traditions of Christendom tell at once under a test like this. Look at old Mounteagle himself, for instance! Ah, you may be as Eastern and esoteric as you like, and weal a turban and a long robe and live on messages from Mahatmas; but if a bit of stone is stolen in your house, and your friends are suspected, you will jolly soon find out that you're an ordinary English gentleman in a fuss. The man who really did it would never want us to think he did it, for he also was an English gentleman. He was also something very much better; he was a Christian thief. I hope and believe he was a penitent thief."

"By your account," said his companion laughing, "the Christian thief and the heathen fraud went by contraries. One was sorry he'd done it and the other was sorry he hadn't."

"We mustn't be too hard on either of them," said Father Brown. "Other English gentlemen have stolen before now, and been covered by legal and political protection; and the West also has its own way of covering theft with sophistry. After all, the ruby is not the only kind of valuable stone in the world that has changed owners; it is true of other precious stones; often carved like cameos and coloured like flowers." The other looked at him inquiringly; and the priest's finger was pointed to the Gothic outline of the great Abbey. "A great graven stone," he said, "and that was also stolen."

IX: THE CHIEF MOURNER OF MARNE

A BLAZE of lightning blanched the grey woods tracing all the wrinkled foliage down to the last curled leaf, as if every detail were drawn in silverpoint or graven in silver. The same strange trick of lightning by which it seems to record millions of minute things in an instant of time, picked out everything, from the elegant litter of the picnic spread under the spreading tree to the pale lengths of winding road, at the end of which a white car was waiting. In the distance a melancholy mansion with four towers like a castle, which in the grey evening had been but a dim and distant huddle of walls like a crumbling cloud, seemed to spring into the foreground, and stood up with all its embattled, roofs and blank and staring windows. And in this, at least, the light had something in it of revelation. For to some of those grouped under the tree that castle was, indeed, a thing faded and almost forgotten, which was to prove its power to spring up again in the foreground of their lives.

The light also clothed for an instant, in the same silver splendour, at least one human figure that stood up as motionless as one of the towers. It was that of a tall man standing on a rise of ground above the rest, who were mostly sitting on the grass or stooping to gather up the hamper and crockery. He wore a picturesque short cloak or cape clasped with a silver clasp and chain, which blazed like a star when the flash touched it; and something metallic in his motionless figure was emphasized by the fact that his closely-curled hair was of the burnished yellow that can be really called gold; and had the look of being younger than his face, which was handsome in a hard aquiline fashion, but looked, under the strong light, a little wrinkled and withered. Possibly it had suffered from wearing a mask of make-up, for Hugo Romaine was the greatest actor of his day. For that instant of illumination the golden curls and ivory mask and silver ornament made his figure gleam like that of a man in armour; the next instant his figure was a dark and even black silhouette against the sickly grey of the rainy evening sky.

But there was something about its stillness, like that of a statue that distinguished it from the group at his feet. All the other figures around him had made the ordinary involuntary movement at the unexpected shock of light; for though the skies were rainy it was the first flash of the storm. The only lady present, whose air of carrying grey hair gracefully, as if she were really proud of it, marked her a matron of the United States, unaffectedly shut her eyes and uttered a sharp cry. Her English husband, General Outram, a very stolid Anglo-Indian, with a bald head and black moustache and whiskers of antiquated pattern, looked up with one stiff movement and then resumed his occupation of tidying up. A young man of the name of Mallow, very big and shy, with brown eyes like a dog's, dropped a cup and apologized awkwardly. A third man, much more dressy, with a resolute head, like an inquisitive terrier's, and grey hair brushed stiffly back, was no other than the great newspaper proprietor, Sir John Cockspur; he cursed freely, but not in an English idiom or accent, for he came from Toronto. But the tall man in the short cloak stood up literally like a statue in the twilight; his eagle face under the full glare had been like the bust of a Roman Emperor, and the carved eyelids had not moved.

A moment after, the dark dome cracked across with thunder, and the statue seemed to come to life. He turned his head over his shoulder and said casually;

"About a minute and half between the flash and the bang, but I think the storm's coming nearer. A tree is not supposed to be a good umbrella for the lightning, but we shall want it soon for the rain. I think it will be a deluge."

The young man glanced at the lady a little anxiously and said: "Can't we get shelter anywhere? There seems to be a house over there."

"There is a house over there," remarked the general, rather grimly; "but not quite what you'd call a hospitable hotel."

"It's curious," said his wife sadly, "that we should be caught in a storm with no house near but that one, of all others."

Something in her tone seemed to check the younger man, who was both sensitive and comprehending; but nothing of that sort daunted the man from Toronto.

"What's the matter with it?" he asked. "Looks rather like a ruin."

"That place," said the general dryly, "belongs to the Marquis of Marne."

"Gee!" said Sir John Cockspur. "I've heard all about that bird, anyhow; and a queer bird, too. Ran him as a front-page mystery in the Comet last year. 'The Nobleman Nobody Knows.'"

"Yes, I've heard of him, too," said young Mallow in a low voice. "There seem to be all sorts of weird stories about why he hides himself like that. I've heard that he wears a mask because he's a leper. But somebody else told me quite seriously that there's a curse on the family; a child born with some frightful deformity that's kept in a dark room."

"The Marquis of Marne has three heads," remarked Romaine quite gravely. "Once in every three hundred years a three-headed nobleman adorns the family tree. No human being dares approach the accursed house except a silent procession of hatters, sent to provide an abnormal number of hats. But," — and his voice took one of those deep and terrible turns, that could cause such a thrill in the theatre — "my friends, those hats are of no human shape."

The American lady looked at him with a frown and a slight air of distrust, as if that trick of voice had moved her in spite of herself.

"I don't like your ghoulish jokes," she said; "and I'd rather you didn't joke about this, anyhow."

"I hear and obey," replied the actor; "but am I, like the Light Brigade, forbidden even to reason why?"

"The reason," she replied, "is that he isn't the Nobleman Nobody Knows. I know him myself, or, at least, I knew him very well when he was an attaché at Washington thirty years ago, when we were all young. And he didn't wear a mask, at least, he didn't wear it with me. He wasn't a leper, though he may he almost as lonely. And he had only one head and only one heart, and that was broken.'

"Unfortunate love affair, of course," said Cockspur. "I should like that for the Comet."

"I suppose it's a compliment to us," she replied thoughtfully, "that you always assume a man's heart is broken by a woman. But there are other kinds of love and bereavement. Have you never read 'In Memoriam'? Have you never heard of David and Jonathan? What broke poor Marne up was the death of his brother; at least, he was really a first cousin, but had been brought up with him like a brother, and was much nearer than most brothers. James Mair, as the marquis was called when I knew him, was the elder of the two, but he always played the part of worshipper, with Maurice Mair as a god. And, by his account, Maurice Mair was certainly a wonder. James was no fool, and very good at his own political job; but it

132

seems that Maurice could do that and everything else; that he was a brilliant artist and amateur actor and musician, and all the rest of it. James was very good-looking himself, long and strong and strenuous, with a high-bridged nose; though I suppose the young people would think he looked very quaint with his beard divided into two bushy whiskers in the fashion of those Victorian times. But Maurice was clean -shaven, and, by the portraits shown to me, certainly quite beautiful; though he looked a little more like a tenor than a gentleman ought to look. James was always asking me again and again whether his friend was not a marvel, whether any woman wouldn't fall in love with him, and so on, until it became rather a bore, except that it turned so suddenly into a tragedy. His whole life seemed to be in that idolatry, and one day the idol tumbled down, and was broken like any china doll. A chill caught at the seaside, and it was all over."

"And after that," asked the young man, "did he shut himself up like this?"

"He went abroad at first," she answered; "away to Asia and the cannibal Islands and Lord knows where. These deadly strokes take different people in different ways. It took him in the way of an utter sundering or severance from everything, even from tradition and as far as possible from memory. He could not bear a reference to the old tie; a portrait or an anecdote or even an association. He couldn't bear the business of a great public funeral. He longed to get away. He stayed away for ten years. I heard some rumour that lie had begun to revive a little at the end of the exile; but when he came back to his own home he relapsed completely. He settled down into religious melancholia, and that's practically madness."

"The priests got hold of him, they say," grumbled the old general. "I know he gave thousands to found a monastery, and lives himself rather like a monk—or, at any rate, a hermit. Can't understand what good they think that will do."

"God darned superstition," snorted Cockspur; "that sort of thing ought to be shown up. Here's a man that might have been useful to the Empire and the world, and these vampires get hold of him and suck him dry. I bet with their unnatural notions they haven't even let him marry."

"No, he has never married," said the lady. "He was engaged when I knew him, as a matter of fact, but I don't think it ever came first with him, and I think it went with the rest when everything else went. Like Hamlet and Ophelia — he lost hold of love because he lost hold of life. But I knew the girl; indeed, I know her still. Between ourselves, it was Viola Grayson, daughter of the old admiral. She's never married either."

"It's infamous! It's infernal!" cried Sir John, bounding up. "It's not only a tragedy, but a crime. I've got a duty to the public, and I mean to see all this nonsensical nightmare. In the twentieth century — —"

He was almost choked with his own protest, and then, after a silence, the old soldier said:

"Well, I don't profess to know much about those things, but I think these religious people need to study a text which says: 'Let the dead bury their dead.'"

"Only, unfortunately, that's just what it looks like," said his wife with a sigh. "It's just like some creepy story of a dead man burying another dead man, over and over again for ever."

"The storm has passed over us," said Romaine, with a rather inscrutable smile. "You will not have to visit the inhospitable house after all."

She suddenly shuddered.

"Oh, I'll never do that again!" she exclaimed.

Mallow was staring at her.

"Again! Have you tried it before?" he cried.

"Well, I did once," she said, with a lightness not without a touch of pride; "but we needn't go back on all that. It's not raining now, but I think we'd better be moving back to the car."

As they moved off in procession, Mallow and the general brought up the rear; and the latter said abruptly, lowering his voice:

"I don't want that little cad Cockspur to hear but as you've asked you'd better know. It's the one thing I can't forgive Marne; but I suppose these monks have drilled him that way. My wife, who had been the best friend he ever had in America, actually came to that house when he was walking in the garden. He was looking at the ground like a monk, and hidden in a black hood that was really as ridiculous as any mask. She had sent her card in, and stood there in his very path. And lie walked past her without a word or a glance, as if she had been a stone. He wasn't human; he was like some horrible automaton. She may well call him a dead man."

"It's all very strange," said the young man rather vaguely. "It isn't like — like what I should have expected."

Young Mr. Mallow, when he left that rather dismal picnic, took himself thoughtfully in search of a friend. He did not know any monks, but he knew one priest, whom he was very much concerned to confront with the curious revelations he had heard that afternoon. He felt he would very much like to know the truth about the cruel superstition that hung over the house of Marne, like the black thundercloud he had seen hovering over it.

After being referred from one place to another, he finally ran his friend Father Brown to earth in the house of another friend, a Roman Catholic friend, with a large family. He entered somewhat abruptly to find Father Brown sitting on the floor with a serious expression, and attempting to pin the somewhat florid hat belonging to a wax doll on to the head of a teddy bear.

Mallow felt a faint sense of incongruity; but he was far too full of his problem to put off the conversation if he could, help it. He was staggering from a sort of set-back in a subconscious process that had been going on for some time. He poured out the whole tragedy of the house of Marne as he had heard it from the general's wife, along with most of the comments of the general and the newspaper proprietor. A new atmosphere of attention seemed to be created with the mention of the newspaper proprietor.

Father Brown neither knew nor cared that his attitudes were comic or commonplace. He continued to sit on the floor, where his large head and short legs made him look very like a baby playing with toys. But there came into his great grey eyes a certain expression that has been seen in the eyes of many men in many centuries through the story of nineteen hundred years; only the men were not generally sitting on floors, but at council tables, or on the seats of chapters, or the thrones of bishops and cardinals; a far-off, watchful look, heavy with the humility of a charge too great for men. Something of that anxious and far-reaching look is found in the eyes of sailors and of those who have steered through so many storms the ship of St. Peter.

"It's very good of you to tell me this," he said. "I'm really awfully grateful, for we may have to do something about it. If it were only people like you and the general, it might be only a private matter; but if Sir John Cockspur is going to spread some sort or scare in his papers — well, he's a Toronto Orangeman, and we can hardly keep out of it."

"But what will you say about it?" asked Mallow anxiously.

"The first thing I should say about it," said Father Brown, "is that, as you tell it, it doesn't sound like life. Suppose, for the sake of argument, that we are all pessimistic vampires blighting all human happiness. Suppose I'm a pessimistic vampire," He scratched his nose with the teddy bear, became faintly conscious of the incongruity, and put it down. "Suppose we do destroy all human and family ties. Why should we entangle a man again in an old family tie just when he showed signs of getting loose from it? Surely it's a little unfair to charge us both with crushing such affection and encouraging such infatuation. I don't see why even a religious maniac should be that particular sort of monomaniac, or how religion could increase that mania, except by brightening it with a little hope."

Then he said, after a pause: "I should like to talk to that general of yours."

"It was his wife who told me," said Mallow.

"Yes," replied the other; "but I'm more interested in what he didn't tell you than in what she did."

"You think he knows more than she does?"

"I think he knows more than she says," answered Father Brown. "You tell me he used a phrase about forgiving everything except the rudeness to his wife. After all, what else was there to forgive?"

Father Brown had risen and shaken his shapeless clothes, and stood looking at the young man with screwed up eyes and slightly quizzical expression. The next moment he had turned, and picking up his equally shapeless umbrella and large shabby hat, went stumping down the street.

He plodded through a variety of wide streets and squares till he came to a handsome old-fashioned house in the West End, where he asked the servant if he could see General Outram. After some little palaver he was shown into a study, fitted out less with books than with maps and globes, where the bald-headed, black-whiskered Anglo-Indian sat smoking a long, thin, black cigar and playing with pins on a chart.

"I am sorry to intrude," said the priest, "and all the more because I can't help the intrusion looking like interference. I want to speak to you about a private matter, but only in the hope of keeping it private. Unfortunately, some people are likely to make it public. I think, general, that you know Sir John Cockspur."

The mass of black moustache and whisker served as a sort of mask for the lower half of the old general's face; it was always hard to see whether he smiled, but his brown eyes often had a certain twinkle.

"Everybody knows him, I suppose," he said. "I don't know him very well.."

"Well, you know everybody knows whatever he knows," said Father Brown, smiling, "when he thinks it convenient to print it. And I understand from my friend Mr. Mallow, whom, I think, you know, that Sir John is going to print some scorching anti-clerical articles founded on what he would call the Marne Mystery. "Monks Drive Marquis Mad,' etc."

"If he is," replied the general, "I don't see why you should come to me about it. I ought to tell you I'm a strong Protestant."

"I'm very fond of strong Protestants," said Father Brown. "I came to you because I was sure you would tell the truth. I hope it is not uncharitable to feel less sure of Sir John Cockspur."

The brown eyes twinkled again, but the general said nothing.

"General," said Father Brown, "suppose Cockspur or his sort were going to make the world ring with tales against your country and your flag. Suppose he said your regiment ran away in battle, or your staff were in the pay of the enemy. Would you let anything stand between you and the facts that would refute him? Wouldn't you get on the track of the truth at all costs to anybody? Well, I have a regiment, and I belong to an army. It is being discredited by what I am certain is a fictitious story; but I don't know the true story. Can you blame me for trying to find it out?"

The soldier was silent, and the priest continued:

"I have heard the story Mallow was told yesterday, about Marne retiring with a broken heart through the death of his more than brother. I am sure there was more in it than that. I came to ask you if you know any more."

"No," said the general shortly; "I cannot tell you any more."

"General," said Father Brown with a broad grin, "you would have called me a Jesuit if I had used that equivocation."

The soldier laughed gruffly, and then growled with much greater hostility.

"Well, I won't tell you, then," he said. "What do you say to that?"

"I only say," said the priest mildly, "that in that case I shall have to tell you."

The brown eyes stared at him; but there was no twinkle in them now. He went on:

"You compel me to state, less sympathetically perhaps than you could, why it is obvious that there is more behind. I am quite sure the marquis has better cause for his brooding and secretiveness than merely having lost an old friend. I doubt whether priests have anything to do with it; I don't even know if he's a convert or merely a man comforting his conscience with charities; but I'm sure he's something more than a chief mourner. Since you insist, I will tell you one or two of the things that made me think so.

"First, it was stated that James Mair was engaged to be married, but somehow became unattached again after the death of Maurice Mair. Why should an honourable man break off his engagement merely because he was depressed by the death of a third party? He's much more likely to have turned for consolation to it; but, anyhow, he was bound in decency to go through with it."

The general was biting his black moustache, and his brown eyes had become very watchful and even anxious, but he did not answer.

"A second point," said Father Brown, frowning at the table. "James Mair was always asking his lady friend whether his cousin Maurice was not very fascinating, and whether women would not admire him. I don't know if it occurred to the lady that there might be another meaning to that inquiry."

The general got to his feet and began to walk or stamp about the room.

"Oh, damn it all," he said, but without any air of animosity.

"The third point," went on Father Brown, "is James Mair's curious manner of mourning—destroying all relics, veiling all portraits, and so on. It does sometimes happen, I admit; it might mean mere affectionate bereavement. But it might mean something else."

"Confound you," said the other. "How long are you going on piling this up?"

"The fourth and fifth points are pretty conclusive," said the priest calmly, "especially if you take them together. The first is that Maurice Mair seems to have had no funeral in particular, considering he was a cadet of a great family. He must have been buried hurriedly; perhaps secretly. And the last point is, that James Mair instantly disappeared to foreign parts; fled, in fact, to the ends of the earth.

"And so," he went on, still in the same soft voice, "when you would blacken my religion to brighten the story of the pure and perfect affection of two brothers, it seems — — "

"Stop!" cried Outram in a tone like a pistol shot. "I must tell you more, or you will fancy worse. Let me tell you one thing to start with. It was a fair fight."

"Ah," said Father Brown, and seemed to exhale a huge breath.

"It was a duel," said the other. "It was probably the last duel fought in England, and it is long ago now."

"That's better," said Father Brown. "Thank God; that's a great deal better."

"Better than the ugly things you thought of, I suppose?" said the general gruffly. "Well, it's all very well for you to sneer at the pure and perfect affection; but it was true for all that. James Mair really was devoted to his cousin, who'd grown up with him like a younger brother. Elder brothers and sisters do sometimes devote themselves to a child like that, especially when he's a sort of infant phenomenon. But James Mair was the sort of simple character in whom even hate is in a sense unselfish. I mean that even when his tenderness turns to rage it is still objective, directed outwards to its object; he isn't conscious of himself. Now poor Maurice Mair was just the opposite. He was far more friendly and popular; but his success had made him live in a house of mirrors. He was first in every sort of sport and art and accomplishment; he nearly always won and took his winning amiably. But if ever, by any chance, he lost, there was just a glimpse of something not so amiable; he was a little jealous. I needn't tell you the whole miserable story of how he was a little jealous of his cousin's engagement; how he couldn't keep his restless vanity from interfering. It's enough to say that one of the few things in which James Mair was admittedly ahead of him was marksmanship with a pistol; and with that the tragedy ended."

"You mean the tragedy began," replied the priest. "The tragedy of the survivor. I thought he did not need any monkish vampires to make him miserable."

"To my mind he's more miserable than he need be," said the general. "After all, as I say, it was a ghastly tragedy, but it was a fair fight. And Jim had great provocation."

"How do you know all this?" asked the priest.

"I know it because I saw it," answered Outram stolidly. "I was James Mair's second, and I saw Maurice Mair shot dead on the sands before my very eyes."

"I wish you would tell me more about it," said Father Brown reflectively. "Who was Maurice Mair's second?"

"He had a more distinguished backing," replied the general grimly. "Hugo Romaine was his second; the great actor, you know. Maurice was mad on acting and had taken up Romaine (who was then a rising but still a struggling man), and financed the fellow and his ventures in return for taking lessons from the professional in his own hobby of amateur acting. But Romaine was then, I suppose, practically dependent on his rich friend; though he's richer now than any aristocrat. So his serving as second proves very little about what he thought of the quarrel. They fought in the English fashion, with only one second apiece; I wanted at least to have a surgeon, but Maurice boisterously refused it, saying the fewer people who knew, the better; and at the worst we could immediately get help. 'There's a doctor in the village not half a mile away,' he said; 'I know him and he's got the fastest horse in the country. He could be brought here in no time; but there's no need to bring him here till we know.' Well, we all knew that Maurice ran most risk, as the pistol was not his weapon; so when he refused aid nobody liked to ask for it. The duel was fought on a flat stretch of sand on the east coast of Scotland; and both the sight and sound of it were masked from the hamlets inland by a long rampart of sandhills patched with rank grass; probably part of the links, though in those days no Englishman had heard of golf. There was one deep, crooked cranny in the sandhills through which we came out on the sands. I can see them now; first a wide strip of dead yellow, and beyond, a narrower strip of dark red; a dark red that seemed already like the long shadow of a deed of blood.

"The thing itself seemed to happen with horrible speed; as if a whirlwind had struck the sand. With the very crack of sound Maurice Mair seemed to spin like a teetotum and pitch upon his face like a ninepin. And queerly enough, while I'd been worrying about him up to that moment, the instant he was dead all my pity was for the man who killed him; as it is to this day and hour. I knew that with that, the whole huge terrible pendulum of my friend's life-long love would swing back; and that whatever cause others might find to pardon him, he would never pardon himself for ever and ever. And so, somehow, the really vivid thing, the picture that burns in my memory so that I can't forget it, is not that of the catastrophe, the smoke and the flash and the falling figure. That seemed to be all over, like the noise that wakes a man up. What I saw, what I shall always see, is poor Jim hurrying across towards his fallen friend and foe; his brown beard looking black against the ghastly pallor of his face, with its high features cut out against the sea; and the frantic gestures with which he waved me to run for the surgeon in the hamlet behind the sandhills. He had dropped his pistol as he ran; he had a glove in one hand and the loose and fluttering fingers of it seemed to elongate and emphasize his wild pantomime of pointing or hailing for help. That is the picture that really remains with me; and there is nothing else in that picture, except the striped background of sands and sea and the dark, dead body lying still as a stone, and the dark figure of the dead man's second standing grim and motionless against the horizon."

"Did Romaine stand motionless?" asked the priest. "I should have thought he would have run even quicker towards the corpse."

"Perhaps he did when I had left," replied the general. "I took in that undying picture in an instant and the next instant I had dived among the sandhills, and was far out of sight of the others. Well, poor Maurice had made a good choice in the matter of doctors; though the doctor came too late, he came quicker than I should have thought possible. This village surgeon was a very remarkable man, red-haired, irascible, but extraordinarily strong in promptitude and presence of mind. I saw him but for a flash as he leapt on his horse and went thundering away to the scene of death, leaving me far behind. But in that flash I had so strong a sense of his personality that I wished to God he had really been called in before the duel began; for I believe on my soul he would have prevented it somehow."

As it was, he cleaned up the mess with marvellous swiftness; long before I could trail back to the sea-shore on my two feet his impetuous practicality had managed everything; the corpse was temporarily buried in the sandhills and the unhappy homicide had been persuaded to do the only thing he could do — to flee for his life. He slipped along the coast till he came to a port and managed to get out of the country. You know the rest; poor Jim remained abroad for many years; later, when the whole thing had been hushed up or forgotten, he returned to his dismal castle and automatically inherited the title. I have never seen him from that day to this, and yet I know what is written in red letters in the inmost darkness of his brain."

"I understand," said Father Brown, "that some of you have made efforts to see him?"

"My wife never relaxed her efforts," said the general. "She refuses to admit that such a crime ought to cut a man off for ever; and I confess I am inclined to agree with her. Eighty years before it would have been thought quite normal; and really it was manslaughter rather than murder. My wife is a great friend of the unfortunate lady who was the occasion of the quarrel and she has an idea that if Jim would consent to see Viola Grayson once again, and receive her assurance that old quarrels are buried, it might restore his sanity. My wife is calling a sort of council of old friends to-morrow, I believe. She is very energetic."

Father Brown was playing with the pins that lay beside the general's map; he seemed to listen rather absent-mindedly. He had the sort of mind that sees things in pictures; and the picture which had coloured even the prosaic mind of the practical soldier took on tints yet more significant and sinister in the more mystical mind of the priest. He saw the dark-red desolation of sand, the very hue of Aceldama, and the dead man lying in a dark heap, and the slayer, stooping as he ran, gesticulating with a glove in demented remorse, and always his imagination came back to the third thing that he could not yet fit into any human picture: the second of the slain man standing motionless and mysterious, like a dark statue on the edge of the sea. It might seem to some a detail; but for him it was that stiff figure that stood up like a standing note of interrogation.

Why had not Romaine moved instantly? It was the natural thing for a second to do, in common humanity, let alone friendship. Even if there were some double-dealing or darker motive not yet understood, one would think it would be done for the sake of appearances. Anyhow, when the thing was all over, it would be natural for the second to stir long before the other second had vanished beyond the sandhills.

"Docs this man Romanic move very slowly?" he asked.

"It's queer you should ask that," answered. Outram, with a sharp glance. "No, as a matter of fact he moves very quickly when he moves at all. But, curiously enough, I was just thinking that only this afternoon I saw him stand exactly like that, during the thunderstorm. He stood in that silver-clasped cape of his, and with one hand on his hip, exactly and in every line as he stood on those bloody sands long ago. The lightning blinded us all, but he did not blink. When it was dark again he was standing there still."

"I suppose he isn't standing there now?" inquired Father Brown. "I mean, I suppose he moved sometime?"

"No, he moved quite sharply when the thunder came," replied the other. "He seemed to have been waiting for it, for he told us the exact time of the interval. Is anything the matter?"

"I've pricked myself with one of your pins," said Father Brown. "I hope I haven't damaged it." But his eyes had snapped and his mouth abruptly shut.

"Are you ill?" inquired the general, staring at him.

"No," answered the priest; "I'm only not quite so stoical as your friend Romaine. I can't help blinking when I see light."

He turned to gather up his hat and umbrella; but when he had got to the door he seemed to remember something and turned back. Coming up close to Outram, he gazed up into his face with a rather helpless expression, as of a dying fish, and made a motion as if to hold him by the waistcoat.

"General," he almost whispered, "for God's sake don't let your wife and that other woman insist on seeing Marne again. Let sleeping dogs lie, or you'll unleash all the hounds of hell."

The general was left alone with a look of bewilderment in his brown eyes, as he sat down again to play with his pins.

Even greater, however, was the bewilderment which attended the successive stages of the benevolent conspiracy of the general's wife, who had assembled her little group of sympathizers to storm the castle of the misanthrope. The first surprise she encountered was the unexplained absence of one of the actors in the ancient tragedy. When they assembled by agreement at a quiet hotel quite near the castle, there was no sign of Hugo Romaine, until a belated telegram from a lawyer told them that the great actor had suddenly left the country. The second surprise, when they began the bombardment by sending up word to the castle with an urgent request for an interview, was the figure which came forth from those gloomy gates to receive the deputation in the name of the noble owner. It was no such figure as they would have conceived suitable to those sombre avenues or those almost feudal formalities. It was not some stately steward or major-domo, nor even a dignified butler or tall and ornamental footman. The only figure that came out of the cavernous castle doorway was the short and shabby figure of Father Brown.

"Look here," he said, in his simple, bothered fashion. "I told you you'd much better leave him alone. He knows what he's doing and it'll only make everybody unhappy."

Lady Outram, who was accompanied by a tall and quietly-dressed lady, still very handsome, presumably the original Miss Grayson, looked at the little priest with cold contempt.

"Really, sir," she said; "this is a very private occasion, and I don't understand what you have to do with it.'

"Trust a priest to have to do with a private occasion," snarled Sir John Cockspur. "Don't you know they live behind the scenes like rats behind a wainscot burrowing their way into everybody's private rooms. See how he's already in possession of poor Marne." Sir John was slightly sulky, as his aristocratic friends had persuaded him to give up the great scoop of publicity in return for the privilege of being really inside a Society secret. It never occurred to him to ask himself whether he was at all like a rat in a wainscot.

"Oh, that's all right," said Father Brown, with the impatience of anxiety. "I've talked it over with the marquis and the only priest he's ever had anything to do with; his clerical tastes have been much exaggerated. I tell you he knows what he's about; and I do implore you all to leave him alone."

"You mean to leave him to this living death of moping and going mad in a ruin!" cried Lady Outram, in a voice that shook a little. "And all because he had the bad luck to shoot a man in a duel more than a quarter of a century ago. Is that what you call Christian charity?"

"Yes," answered the priest stolidly; "that is what I call Christian charity."

"It's about all the Christian charity you'll ever get out of these priests," cried Cockspur bitterly. "That's their only idea of pardoning a poor fellow for a piece of folly; to wall him up alive and starve him to death with fasts and penances and pictures of hell-fire. And all because a bullet went wrong."

"Really, Father Brown," said General Outram, "do you honestly think he deserves this? Is that your Christianity?"

"Surely the true Christianity," pleaded his wife more gently, "is that which knows all and pardons all; the love that can remember — and forget."

"Father Brown," said young Mallow, very earnestly, "I generally agree with what you say; but I'm hanged if I can follow you here. A shot in a duel, followed instantly by remorse, is not such an awful offence."

"I admit." said Father Brown dully, "that I take a more serious view of his offence."

"God soften your hard heart," said the strange lady speaking for the first time. "I am going to speak to my old friend."

Almost as if her voice had raised a ghost in that great grey house, something stirred within and a figure stood in the dark doorway at the top of the great stone flight of steps. It was clad in dead black, but there was something wild about the blanched hair and something in the pale features that was like the wreck of a marble statue.

Viola Grayson began calmly to move up the great flight of steps; and Outram muttered in his thick black moustache: "He won't cut her dead as he did my wife, I fancy."

Father Brown, who seemed in a collapse of resignation, looked up at him for a moment.

"Poor Marne has enough on his conscience," he said. "Let us acquit him of what we can. At least he never cut your wife."

"What do you mean by that?"

"He never knew her," said Father Brown.

As they spoke, the tall lady proudly mounted the last step and came face to face with the Marquis of Marne. His lips moved, but something happened before he could speak.

A scream rang across the open space and went wailing away in echoes along those hollow walls. By the abruptness and agony with which it broke from the woman's lips it might have been a mere inarticulate cry. But it was an articulated word; and they all heard it with a horrible distinctness.

"Maurice!"

"What is it, dear?" cried Lady Outram, and began to run up the steps; for the other woman was swaying as if she might fall down the whole stone flight. Then she faced about and began to descend, all bowed and shrunken and shuddering. "Oh, my God," she was saying. "Oh, my God, it isn't Jim at all. It's Maurice!"

"I think, Lady Outram," said the priest gravely, "you had better go with your friend."

As they turned, a voice fell on them like a stone from the top of the stone stair, a voice that might have come out of an open grave. It was hoarse and unnatural, like the voices of men who are left alone with wild birds on desert islands. It was the voice of the Marquis of Marne, and it said: "Stop!"

"Father Brown," he said, "before your friends disperse I authorize you to tell them all I have told you. Whatever follows, I will hide from it no longer."

"You are right," said the priest, "and it shall be counted to you."

"Yes," said Father Brown quietly to the questioning company afterwards. "He has given me the right to speak; but I will not tell it as he told me, but as I found it out for myself. Well, I knew from the first that the blighting monkish influence was all nonsense out of novels. Our people might possibly, in certain cases, encourage a man to go regularly into a monastery, but certainly not to hang about in a mediaeval castle. In the same way, they certainly wouldn't want him to dress up as a monk when he wasn't a monk. But it struck me that he might himself want to wear a monk's hood or even a mask. I had heard of him as a mourner, and then as a murderer; but already I had hazy suspicions that his reason for hiding might not only be concerned with what lie was, but with who he was.

"Then came the general's vivid description of the duel; and the most vivid thing in it to me was the figure of Mr. Romaine in the background; it

146

was vivid because it was in the background. Why did the general leave behind him on the sand a dead man, whose friend stood yards away from him like a stock or a stone? Then I heard something, a mere trifle, about a trick habit that Romaine has of standing quite still when he is waiting for something to happen; as he waited for the thunder to follow the lightning. Well, that automatic trick in this case betrayed everything. Hugo Romaine on that old occasion, also, was waiting for something."

"But it was all over," said the general. "What could he have been waiting for?"

"He was waiting for the duel," said Father Brown.

"But I tell you I saw the duel!" cried the general.

"And I tell you, you didn't see the duel," said the priest.

"Are you mad?" demanded the other. "Or why should you think I am blind?"

"Because you were blinded — that you might not see," said the priest. "Because you are a good man and God had mercy on your innocence, and he turned your face away from that unnatural strife. He set a wall of sand and silence between you and what really happened on that horrible red shore, abandoned to the raging spirits of Judas and of Cain."

"Tell us what happened!" gasped the lady impatiently.

"I will tell it as I found it," proceeded the priest. "The next thing I found was that Romaine the actor had been training Maurice Mair in all the tricks of the trade of acting. I once had a friend who went in for acting. He gave me a very amusing account of how his first week's training consisted entirely of falling down; of learning how to fall flat without a stagger, as if he were stone dead."

"God have mercy on us!" cried the general, and gripped the arms of his chair as if to rise.

"Amen," said Father Brown. "You told me how quickly it seemed to come; in fact, Maurice fell before the bullet flew, and lay perfectly still, waiting. And his wicked friend and teacher stood also in the background, waiting."

"We are waiting," said Cockspur, "and I feel as if I couldn't wait."

"James Mair, already broken with remorse, rushed across to the fallen man and bent over to lift him up. He had thrown away his pistol like an unclean thing; but Maurice's pistol still lay under his hand and it was undischarged. Then as the elder man bent over the younger, the younger lifted himself on his left arm and shot the elder through the body. He knew he was not so good a shot, but there was no question of missing the heart at that distance."

The rest of the company had risen and stood staring down at the narrator with pale faces. "Are you sure of this?" asked Sir John at last, in a thick voice.

"I am sure of it," said Father Brown, "and now I leave Maurice Mair, the present Marquis of Marne, to your Christian charity. You have told me something to-day about Christian charity. You seemed to me to give it almost too large a place; but how fortunate it is for poor sinners like this man that you err so much on the side of mercy, and are ready to be reconciled to all mankind."

"Hang it all," exploded the general; "if you think I'm going to be reconciled to a filthy viper like that, I tell you I wouldn't say a word to save him from hell. I said I could pardon a regular decent duel, but of all the treacherous assassins — — "

"He ought to be lynched," cried Cockspur excitedly. "He ought to burn alive like a nigger in the States. And if there is such a thing as burning for ever, he jolly well — — "

"I wouldn't touch him with a barge-pole myself," said Mallow.

"There is a limit to human charity," said Lady Outram, trembling all over.

"There is," said Father Brown dryly; "and that is the real difference between human charity and Christian charity. You must forgive me if I was not altogether crushed by your contempt for my uncharitableness to-day; or by the lectures you read me about pardon for every sinner. For it seems to me that you only pardon the sins that you don't really think sinful. You only forgive criminals when they commit what you don't regard as crimes, but rather as conventions. So you tolerate a conventional duel, just as you tolerate a conventional divorce. You forgive because there isn't anything to be forgiven."

"But, hang it all," cried Mallow, "you don't expect us to be able to pardon a vile thing like this?"

"No," said the priest; "but we have to be able to pardon it."

He stood up abruptly and looked round at them.

"'We have to touch such men, not with a bargepole, but with a benediction," he said. "We have to say the word that will save them from hell. We alone are left to deliver them from despair when your human charity deserts them. Go on your own primrose path pardoning all your favourite vices and being generous to your fashionable crimes; and leave us in the darkness, vampires of the night, to console those who really need consolation; who do things really indefensible, things that neither the world nor they themselves can defend; and none but a priest will pardon. Leave us with the men who commit the mean and revolting and real crimes; mean as St. Peter when the cock crew, and yet the dawn came."

"The dawn," repeated Mallow doubtfully. "You mean hope — for him?"

"Yes," replied the other. "Let me ask you one question. You are great ladies and men of honour and secure of yourselves; you would never, you can tell yourselves, stoop to such squalid reason as that. But tell me this. If any of you had so stooped, which of you, years afterwards, when you were old and rich and safe, would have been driven by conscience or confessor to tell such a story of yourself? You say you could not commit so base a crime. Could you confess so base a crime?" The others gathered their possessions together and drifted by twos and threes out of the room in silence. And Father Brown, also in silence, went back to the melancholy castle of Marne.

X: THE SECRET OF FLAMBEAU

" — the sort of murders in which I played the part of the murderer," said Father Brown, putting down the wineglass. The row of red pictures of crime had passed before him in that moment.

"It is true," he resumed, after a momentary pause, "that somebody else had played the part of the murderer before me and done me out of the actual experience. I was a sort of understudy; always in a state of being ready to act the assassin. I always made it my business, at least, to know the part thoroughly. What I mean is that, when I tried to imagine the state of mind in which such a thing would be done, I always realized that I might have done it myself under certain mental conditions, but not under others; and not generally under the obvious ones. And then, of course, I knew who really had done it; and he was not generally the obvious person.

"For instance, it seemed obvious to say that the revolutionary poet had killed the old judge who saw red about red revolutionaries. But that isn't really a reason for the revolutionary poet killing him. It isn't, if you think what it would really be like to be a revolutionary poet. Now I set myself conscientiously down to be a revolutionary poet. I mean that particular sort of pessimistic anarchial lover of revolt, not as reform, but rather as destruction. I tried to clear my mind of such elements of sanity and constructive common sense as I have had the luck to learn or inherit. I shut down and darkened all the skylights through which comes the good daylight out of heaven; I imagined a mind lit only by a red light from below; a fire rending rocks and cleaving abysses upwards. And even with the vision at its wildest and worst, I could not see why such a visionary should cut short his own career by colliding with a common policeman, for killing one out of a million conventional old fools, as he would have called them. He wouldn't do it; however much he wrote songs of violence. He wouldn't do it, because he wrote songs of violence. A man who can express himself in song need not express himself in suicide. A poem was an event to him; and he would want to have more of them. Then I thought of another sort of heathen; the sort that is not destroying the world but entirely depending on the world. I thought that, save for the grace of God, I might have been a man for whom the world was a blaze of electric lights, with nothing but utter darkness beyond and around it. The worldly man, who really lives only for this world and believes in no other, whose worldly success and pleasure are all he can ever snatch out of nothingness—that is the man who will really do anything, when he is in danger of losing the whole world and saving nothing. It is not the revolutionary man but the respectable man who would commit any crime—to save his respectability. Think what exposure would mean to a man like that fashionable barrister; and exposure of the one crime still really hated by his fashionable world— treason against patriotism. If I had been in his position, and had nothing better than his philosophy, heaven alone knows what I might have done. That is just where this little religious exercise is so wholesome."

"Some people would think it was rather morbid," said Grandison Chace dubiously.

"Some people," said Father Brown gravely, "undoubtedly do think that charity and humility are morbid. Our friend the poet probably would. But I'm not arguing those questions; I'm only trying to answer your question about how I generally go to work. Some of your countrymen have apparently done me the honour to ask how I managed to frustrate a few miscarriages of justice. Well, you can go back and tell them that I do it by morbidity. But I most certainly don't want them to think I do it by magic."

Chace continued to look at him with a reflective frown; he was too intelligent not to understand the idea; he would also have said that he was too healthy-minded to like it. He felt as if he were talking to one man and yet to a hundred murderers. There was something uncanny about that very small figure, perched like a goblin beside the goblin stove; and the sense that its round head had held such a universe of wild unreason and imaginative injustice. It was as if the vast void of dark behind it were a throng of dark gigantic figures, the ghosts of great criminals held at bay by the magic circle of the red stove, but ready to tear their master in pieces.

"Well, I'm afraid I do think it's morbid," he said frankly. "And I'm not sure it isn't almost as morbid as magic. But morbidity or no, there's one thing to be said; it must be an interesting experience." Then he added, after reflection: "I don't know whether you would make a really good criminal. But you ought to make a rattling good novelist."

"I only have to deal with real events," said Father Brown. "But it's sometimes harder to imagine real things than unreal ones."

"Especially," said the other, "when they are the great crimes of the world."

"It's not the great crimes but the small crimes that are really hard to imagine," replied the priest.

"I don't quite know what you mean by that," said Chace.

"I mean commonplace crimes like stealing jewels," said Father Brown; "like that affair of the emerald necklace or the Ruby of Meru or the artificial goldfish. The difficulty in those cases is that you've got to make your mind small. High and mighty humbugs, who deal in big ideas, don't do those obvious things. I was sure the Prophet hadn't taken the ruby; or the Count the goldfish; though a man like Bankes might easily take the emeralds. For them, a jewel is a piece of glass: and they can see through the glass. But the little, literal people take it at its market value.

"For that you've got to have a small mind. It's awfully hard to get; like focusing smaller and sharper in a wobbling camera. But some things helped; and they threw a lot of light on the mystery, too. For instance, the sort of man who brags about having 'shown up' sham magicians or poor quacks of any sort — he's always got a small mind. He is the sort of man who 'sees through' tramps and trips them up in telling lies. I dare say it might sometimes be a painful duty. It's an uncommonly base pleasure. The moment I realized what a small mind meant, I knew where to look for it — in the man who wanted to expose the Prophet — and it was he that sneaked the ruby; in the man who jeered at his sister's psychic fancies — and it was he who nabbed the emeralds. Men like that always have their eye on jewels; they never could rise, with the higher humbugs, to despising jewels. Those criminals with small minds are always quite conventional. They become criminals out of sheer conventionality.

"It takes you quite a long time to feel so crudely as that, though. It's quite a wild effort of imagination to be so conventional. To want one potty little object as seriously as all that. But you can do it. ... You can get nearer to it. Begin by thinking of being a greedy child; of how you might have stolen a sweet in a shop; of how there was one particular sweet you wanted then you must subtract the childish poetry; shut off the fairy light that shone on the sweet-stuff shop; imagine you really think you know the world and the market value of sweets you contract your mind like the camera focus, the thing shapes and then sharpens ... and then, suddenly, it comes!"

He spoke like a man who had once captured a divine vision. Grandison Chace was still looking at him with a frown of mingled mystification and interest. It must be confessed that there did flash once beneath his heavy frown a look of something almost like alarm. It was as if the shock of the first strange confession of the priest still thrilled faintly through him like the last vibration of a thunderclap in the room. Under the surface he was saying to himself that the mistake had only been a temporary madness; that, of course. Father Brown could not really be the monster and murderer he had beheld for that blinding and bewildering instant. But was there not something wrong with the man who talked in that calm way about being a murderer? Was it possible that the priest was a little mad?

"Don't you think," he said, abruptly; "that this notion of yours, of a man trying to feel like a criminal, might make him a little too tolerant of crime?"

Father Brown sat up and spoke in a more staccato style.

"I know it does just the opposite. It solves the whole problem of time and sin. It gives a man his remorse beforehand."

There was a silence; the American looked at the high and steep roof that stretched half across the enclosure; his host gazed into the fire without moving; and then the priest's voice came on a different note, as if from lower down.

"There are two ways of renouncing the devil," he said; "and the difference is perhaps the deepest chasm in modem religion. One is to have a horror of him because he is so far off; and the other to have it because he is so near. And no virtue and vice are so much divided as those two virtues."

They did not answer and he went on in the same heavy tone, as if he were dropping words like molten lead.

"You may think a crime horrible because you could never commit it. I think it horrible because I could commit it. You think of it as something like an eruption of Vesuvius; but that would not really be so terrible as this house catching fire. If a criminal suddenly appeared in this room— —"

"If a criminal appeared in this room," said Chace, smiling, "I think you would be a good deal too favourable to him. Apparently you would start by telling him that you were a criminal yourself and explaining how perfectly natural it was that he should have picked his father's pocket or cut his mother's throat. Frankly, I don't think it's practical. I think that the practical effect would be that no criminal would ever reform. It's easy enough to theorize and take hypothetical cases; but we all know we're only talking in the air. Sitting here in M. Duroc's nice, comfortable house, conscious of our respectability and all the rest of it, it just gives us a theatrical thrill to talk about thieves and murderers and the mysteries of their souls. But the people who really have to deal with thieves and murderers have to deal with them differently. We are safe by the fireside; and we know the house is not on fire. We know there is not a criminal in the room."

The M. Duroc to whom allusion had been made rose slowly from what had been called his fireside, and his huge shadow flung from the fire seemed to cover everything and darken even the very night above him.

"There is a criminal in this room," he said. "I am one. I am Flambeau, and the police of two hemispheres are still hunting for me."

The American remained gazing at him with eyes of a stony brightness; he seemed unable to speak or move.

"There is nothing mystical, or metaphorical, or vicarious about my confession," said Flambeau. "I stole for twenty years with these two hands; I fled from the police on these two feet. I hope you will admit that my activities were practical. I hope you will admit that my judges and pursuers really had to deal with crime. Do you think I do not know all about their way of reprehending it? Have I not heard the sermons of the righteous and seen the cold stare of the respectable; have I not been lectured in the lofty and distant style, asked how it was possible for anyone to fall so low, told that no decent person could ever have dreamed of such depravity? Do you think all that ever did anything but make me laugh? Only my friend told me that he knew exactly why I stole; and I have never stolen since."

Father Brown made a gesture as of deprecation; and Grandison Chace at last let out a long breath like a whistle.

"I have told you the exact truth," said Flambeau; "and it is open to you to hand me over to the police."

There was an instant of profound stillness, in which could be faintly heard the belated laughter of Flambeau's children in the high, dark house above them, and the crunching and snorting of the great, grey pigs in the twilight. And then it was cloven by a high voice, vibrant and with a touch of offence, almost surprising for those who do not understand the sensitive American spirit, and how near, in spite of commonplace contrasts, it can sometimes come to the chivalry of Spain.

"Monsieur Duroc." he said rather stiffly. "We have been friends, I hope, for some considerable period; and I should be pretty much pained to suppose you thought me capable of playing you such a trick while I was enjoying your hospitality and the society of your family, merely because you chose to tell me a little of your own autobiography of your own free will. And when you spoke merely in defence of your friend — no, sir, I can't imagine any gentleman double-crossing another under such circumstances; it would be a damned sight better to be a dirty informer and sell men's blood for money. But in a case like this — —! Could you conceive any man being such a Judas?"

"I could try," said Father Brown.

Printed by Amazon Italia Logistica S.r.l.
Torrazza Piemonte (TO), Italy

41347035R00091